SHATTERED NIGHT

Book Four in THE EXTRACTION LIST Series

BY RENEE N. MELAND

SHATTERED NIGHT

Copyright © 2018 by Renee N. Meland.
All rights reserved.
First Print Edition: October 2018

Limitless Publishing, LLC
Kailua, HI 96734
www.limitlesspublishing.com

Formatting: Limitless Publishing

ISBN-13: 978-1-64034-455-6
ISBN-10: 1-64034-455-1

No part of this book may be reproduced, scanned, or distributed in any printed or electronic form without permission. Please do not participate in or encourage piracy of copyrighted materials in violation of the author's rights. Thank you for respecting the hard work of this author.

This is a work of fiction. Names, characters, places, and incidents either are the product of the author's imagination or are used fictitiously, and any resemblance to locales, events, business establishments, or actual persons—living or dead—is entirely coincidental.

Dedication

To My Readers:

Thank you for your time, your enthusiasm, and your encouragement

CHAPTER ONE

Riley

Contrary to popular belief, I am certain that the world *can* stop turning. I felt it in my blood, flesh, and bones on the afternoon that changed everything—the exact minute where I knew nothing would ever go back to the way it was.

Apparently, Cain was not the only person who could stop my heart and start it back up again. Because when I realized who was standing in front of us, my heart became still in my chest. The person whose roof we were under, and who at that moment could decide to have his personal army dispatch us if we so much as blinked wrong, was Officer Marcus Keegan, the man who had nearly beaten Cain to death as a boy. He was now living under a new identity, General Cole, savior to every citizen in his personal makeshift village. His hair was different, cut close to his scalp. His eye color was now different from before and his face had, of course, become worn with age, but there he was:

alive, well, and in charge. And if that wasn't bad enough, he had his arm around my mother. Worse than that, she was smiling.

I inhaled to speak, but before the words could get out ("you son of a bitch, you bastard, we're leaving right this minute" came to mind), Cain cut me off with a raspy breath from his bed. "Thank you for having us, General Cole. We are very lucky to be here." Hearing Cain grovel was not something I was accustomed to, and it made me sick. I looked between him and Jordyn, praying that one of them would somehow explain to me what we were still doing there. I hoped some secret exchange between them would tell me how we would get out of the mess we were in, but I saw nothing. For all we knew, it was a poison that Keegan had pumping through the bag hooked to Cain's arm, not fluids at all. An image flashed through my head of Cain suddenly going white, blood sputtering from his lips before his breath gave out for the last time.

When Cain was out of Keegan's line of sight, he subtly shook his head at me, willing me to keep my mouth shut. Seeing that I was having trouble doing just that, Jordyn did what Cain couldn't and came over to me. Though I could tell she shared my feelings, she was doing a better job at hiding them. She threw her arm around me and softly whispered in my ear, "Not the time. Not yet."

If not now, when? This may be the only chance we have.

To my disgust, Keegan left my mother's side and came toward us, grinning like we were just two neighbors making each other's acquaintance in a long-lost suburbia, square houses protruding from the earth one right after the other, a sight that had disappeared from the American landscape long ago and had no place in the new world. He gently kissed us both on the cheeks, letting his lips linger there for an excruciatingly long moment. The cold softness of Keegan's lips seemed to stay on my cheek long after he had released me. Jordyn's eyes closed for just a second too long and I knew she was trying to forget his touch too. Dominic came over and slid himself in between Keegan and us, hardened expression comforting me during all our acting. I couldn't help but smile seeing the man that had been so close to me for the past few years, with every inch of his body rippling with muscles, standing next to our adversary, making Keegan's slender frame look almost adolescent next to his.

Then I remembered we were standing in his territory—a place where strength was no match for a bullet.

"Well, everyone, I'm sure you have had a long journey. Let's let Cain rest and show you all to your rooms," Keegan said, arm slithering around my mother once again. He touched his large belt buckle with his other hand, and I noticed that it had a deer with a snake in its mouth engraved into the metal. *Fitting that there would be a snake*, I thought. Everyone but Dom, Nick, and I started heading toward the door of the hospital room.

"No, we can't!" I whispered as I frantically looked at Dom, who stood as firmly as I did.

To my surprise, Jordyn had been leaving with the group heading out into the hallway and had to double back toward us in order to come to speak with me. Keegan was at the front of the group, well out of hearing distance, but she pulled both of us closer to her just in case. "Trust me, guys. We can leave. You know if I thought for a second we couldn't, I'd be standing right next to you."

"But how do you know?"

"You can't be sure he won't kill Cain the minute we leave this room!" Dominic closed and opened his fists rhythmically at his sides in an effort to keep his composure. "There's no way I'm leaving him alone, not again." I knew he could only be referring to the last time Keegan came after Cain, back when Dom was in jail and could do nothing to stop it. The fact that he had somehow found a way to hold himself partially responsible broke my heart, and I saw a flicker of sadness in his eyes that I'd only seen one other time, back when Cain first got shot, and we weren't sure if we'd lost him for good; a father's guilt, nowhere near deserved.

Jordyn's voice was serious. "Trust me, I know this guy. Cain's told me every little detail about him. If he wanted to kill Cain immediately, he would have done it already. Think about it. He called us all here knowing we had nowhere else to go. He's got everyone Cain loves under one roof. The purpose of this whole thing is to watch Cain squirm."

"She's right," I heard Cain's rasp from behind us. He looked at me sympathetically. "I know you're worried, and you should be, but right now, we don't have a choice." He lifted up his arm, tubes extending from it. "I can't leave yet. As much as it kills me, I need his doctors. If I leave here now I'm done for. And if you all tried to leave he'd have no more use for you and kill you where you stand, probably right in front of me." He took a deep breath and swallowed hard, every word robbing him of energy that he didn't have to spare. "So for now, just for now, you have to play along. Pretend I never told you anything, that you have no idea who he really is. His appearance is different enough from how he looked when he was in charge of the Task Force, so that seems possible. That's probably why all the people in the village are living under his leadership. If they did figure out who he was, I'm sure they would do even worse to him than what we would like to do."

"You're right. I didn't notice many older children around when we came in," Dom admitted.

Most of the people in town probably had children who were taken by the Task Force years ago, leaving them wondering what became of them for the rest of their lives. There was no greater thing that would justify revenge than that. I considered if the best move for us would be to just reveal his true identity in the middle of the town square. On the surface, it seemed simple, but we didn't have any proof. It would be Keegan's word against ours, and we were the strangers in an unfamiliar place, not the man who had given them a new life. If we did tell them what we knew and it went badly, we could all see ourselves jailed…or worse. The townspeople could *not* believe our story just as easily as they could, and if they didn't, we would be outnumbered with no weapons to defend ourselves.

"We need to get our bearings and figure out the situation so we can all get out of here alive." Cain turned to Dom, who had parked himself in a chair by his bedside, evidently not letting his argument dissuade his position about leaving him alone. "Dom, you have to pretend that when they beat you up in jail that day, you were too injured to remember faces. You have to act the same as Riley. Pretend you only know him as General Cole." He turned to Nick, who seemed as determined to stay as Dom was. "You were only ten when you met him. He's changed his appearance since then. You have to pretend it worked and that you don't recognize him."

Nick started to pace. "Yeah, that…or I could march right down the hallway and break his neck. That would also work," Nick said.

Cain gave him a knock-it-off stare. "Nick, Dom, you have to go."

Dom shook his head. "I'm not leaving you here. Forget it. It's too risky."

Nick went over and stood at Dom's side. "Me neither."

As much as it killed me, I knew Cain was right.

The best way to stay alive right then was to play along with the ridiculous charade that Keegan called civilization. Though we may have been able to see through it, there were hundreds of people surrounding us that did not. I sighed, glancing sympathetically at Dom and Nick, then said, "Cain, I think it's feasible that one of us stays with you as much as possible, just in case Keegan changes his mind. We can take shifts. I don't think it would be suspicious if you always had one of us with you. We are all concerned about your condition after all. Nothing out of the ordinary about that."

He seemed to think about it for a moment but nodded his approval. I took his hand. "And besides, I don't think there's any way you are getting Dominic out of that chair."

Cain reached up with his free hand and touched my face. "Be careful. You're in the most danger of all of them."

"Why is that?"

"Because I love you so much. If he figures that out, he's going to use that in the worst way possible. You can count on it."

"Well, I see your point. But, from the way he was hanging all over my mother, I doubt he plans on doing anything to me any time soon. She must be useful to him in some way or he wouldn't be bothering."

Cain gave me a look. "That really doesn't make me feel better."

Reluctantly, Nick, Jordyn, and I left the room and ran up to the others, who had already made it down the hallway and around the corner. "Oh, there you are! I'm sure it's hard to leave your friend. But he'll be close by." Keegan's tone sent a shiver up my spine.

"Why?"

He grinned. "Because you all will be staying with me. The top floor in the hospital is living quarters that can house several people." He opened a door on one side of the hall. "Let me see if I remember all these names…" He pointed at each of us. "Jordyn, Olivia, Riley…you will be in here."

He swung open the door and I looked inside the room. To my surprise, it stretched out wide, or at least wider than I was accustomed to. We each had our own bed, made up with perfect white linens and crisp sheets. There were even decorative pillows on top of them.

"Wow! It's like a hotel!" Olivia exclaimed.

I glared at her. If she noticed that Jordyn and I were barely keeping it together, she didn't let on.

Keegan smiled. "I'm so glad you like it!" He nodded toward Nick and Reagan. "You two and Father Dominic will be joining Ford in that room at the end of the hallway.

Ford gestured to Nick and Reagan to follow him. "Come on guys, I'll show you."

"Just to warn you guys, Ford has strange hours, so that'll be something you have to get used to." He patted Ford on the back, and Ford grinned in return for the display of affection like a dog whose owner scratched the fur on his head. "He's one of our best guards. I depend on him a lot."

I tried to hide my disgust. One of my best friends was working for our worst enemy and seemed happy about it. Though he had no idea who Keegan was, the pride in Ford's eyes that came from his compliment made my stomach turn.

I forced myself to speak. "Well…thank you. We need to be getting to bed now. Come on, Mom."

"Oh, honey, I stay, um…somewhere else."

At first, I was confused, but as Keegan grabbed her hand and intertwined her fingers in between his own, like a bug trapped in a spider's web, I knew.

Shattered Night

"Your mother won't be staying here." He kissed her on the cheek. "She will be staying with me, where she has been for quite some time. I'm sure you all would want your privacy anyhow." He looked at my mom. "We understand how valuable privacy can be."

Before I could protest, Jordyn ushered me and Olivia inside and shut the door behind us. She dragged me forward and parked me on the bed farthest from the door. "Oh. My. God! What the hell? She's with him? Him! She knows all about what happened with Keegan and she's still with him. How could she do this? I—"

Olivia cut me off. "Would someone please tell me what the hell is going on?" She sat down beside me and ran her fingers across the bedspread. "Why are we upset that we're living like queens right now? No offense to your little island or whatever but this place seems pretty nice to me." She spread herself across her bed without a care in the world. I knew we had to tell her. Cain wouldn't like someone he didn't get along with to know the horrible experience he went through, but I knew he'd understand given the circumstances.

"Liv, he's not who he says he is. Not by a mile."

She sighed. "What are you talking about now?"

Jordyn and I explained the whole sordid tale to her. As the story went on, her expression became more and more desperate. By the time we were done, her jaw was pretty much on the floor. "And now your mother is sleeping with him? I second what Riley said earlier. No offense, but what is wrong with her?"

Jordyn answered. "Honestly, I don't know. But for now, we have to do what Cain said and play it smart. Riley, don't approach your mother until you are sure you are alone, ok?"

I sat there silently.

"Ok?" She said again, this time more forcefully.

"Fine. You're right. I know you're right. Maybe there's some logical explanation. There has to be."

"There better be," Olivia said. "Otherwise, your mother's sleeping with the enemy, so she's the enemy too."

Jordyn scowled at her. "You could be a little more sensitive for fuck's sake."

"What? I'm just saying what you know is true. If she's with him, we can't trust her either. End of story." She clapped her hands together and made a sweeping gesture as if wiping my mother away like dust.

I looked at Jordyn, hoping she would have a counter-argument that I couldn't think of. She didn't. As much as I hated to admit it, Olivia was right. Until we could talk to her, I knew that any plans we made to get out of there couldn't reach my mother's ears.

After a night of fitful, torturous dreaming with bits of sleep thrown in, Jordyn, Olivia, and I got up and decided we should explore the town as soon as possible. As we were leaving, we ran into Reagan and Ford in the hallway. Reagan was as clueless about Keegan's true identity as Ford, and I was about to fill them in when something in my gut held me back. Jordyn was about to speak, but I quickly squeezed her arm and spoke first. "Where are you guys off to?"

She looked at me, clearly confused, but said nothing.

"Nick's in with Cain and Dom's asleep, so Ford's going to introduce me to some of the other guards. Maybe I'll get to see some cool weapons." Reagan raised his eyebrows in a mischievous expression.

I forced a smile. "Great! Have fun. We'll see you later ok?" I turned away and linked arms with Jordyn and Olivia, pulling them along with me whether they wanted to or not. As we moved out of hearing distance, Jordyn stopped me.

"Why didn't you tell them?"

"Honestly, I don't know."

Olivia stopped walking, yanked herself from my grasp, and looked at me. "Yes, you do. You know that Ford could be just as tainted as your mom. He's working for the guy after all. Best to keep him in the dark too."

"Olivia's right," Jordyn said. "And you know Reagan can't keep anything from Ford. So, let's just encourage Reagan to learn as much as he can about this guard stuff. Once we figure out what to do, he'll probably be able to tell us something useful. For now, it's up to the five of us."

As we opened the door to the outside world, I wondered what new horrors we'd yet to discover awaited. The sight of a peaceful town with happy families obviously rebuilding satisfying lives in the face of a world that had been destroyed was the worst part: our nightmare masked as utopia. And if my own mother could get swept away, what was to keep the rest of our group from being swallowed up right along with her? The heat hit us the minute we stepped outside, the very air itself trying to make us feel trapped in a world where we didn't fit in.

It didn't have to try very hard.

I walked in the middle, flanked by Jordyn and Olivia. "Stay together. We don't know what's out here."

Jordyn agreed and for once, so did Olivia. Our new circumstances seemed to quiet her argumentative nature. In fact, though it could have been imagination, I think she actually stepped slightly closer to me.

I surveyed our surroundings like I had thousands of time before, but now it seemed different, more urgent. Every small canvas tent, every former barracks could be hiding an enemy, and it felt as if every grocery seller could see right through us. I felt the curious gazes falling upon us as a weight, one I wasn't sure I could bear without Cain by my side.

Back at our compound, I felt in control. I was the head of security after all, and Cain had taught me well. But with the anchor of my life lying in a hospital bed, everything seemed off-kilter. Sophie's brother Ben had snatched that from me when he shot Cain, and the rightness inside me hadn't returned. I was supposed to have it together…nothing was supposed to scare me.

But the certainty inside me had been replaced with heightened dread as if every pair of eyes that I passed could spell the death of me, or even worse, the man I loved. I tried my best to block out the sick feeling, taking mental notes of the layout of

Shattered Night

Keegan's village. I noticed that with the abundance of buildings and tents to house the townspeople, it was going to be very difficult for us to do anything without someone noticing. It was as if Keegan had designed it with Cain in mind, taking away one of his best weapons, the ability to hide in the shadows.

The market seemed to be the thickest hub of activity in the town. We could barely stay next to each other as we made our way through the crowd. Children weaved in and out between the produce stands with huge smiles on their faces, teeth glistening in the sun as if they were on a television ad from before things went sideways. Most looked to be around the same age, conceived around the time where their older counterparts were snatched away from their families by the Task Force. I remembered people calling them "battle boomers" in reference to the "baby boomer" generation. But this time, instead of being born of victory, they were conceived after their families had been torn apart. Their smiles made my blood grow cold—the feeling you get where you know someone's happiness is brought about by blissful ignorance.

I noticed something else too. On every light post, and every wall of every building, there were posters, all hand-drawn by someone very talented. There was a man in a guard's uniform saluting with the American flag in the background as he stared off into the distance. There was a banner across the bottom that said, "Every man has value, every man comes first. Be part of our family today, and help protect the generation of tomorrow." Aside from the obvious problem that there is only one "first," it was a lovely sentiment, and judging by how many guards Keegan had under his command, it had worked beautifully. He was skillfully using propaganda at its finest.

And the fact he was succeeding chilled me to the core.

We were about to pass a little store when Jordyn grabbed me by the arm. She pointed inside and gestured for me to follow her gaze. "That guy is selling a lot of different stuff. But do you notice what's nowhere in his store?" I took a visual survey of everything on the shelves. There were spices, dried meats in long, thin strips, meat cut into chunks that were wrapped in paper, pans, tools of every kind…but something was missing.

"Where are the weapons?"

"Exactly." We'd had to turn ours in at the gate but assumed that was because we were newcomers. Jordyn reached down to her empty holster. She had told me that morning she had put it on because she didn't feel right without it, that she didn't feel like herself. But even with it there, the weight of her gun was missing.

We continued our rounds, glancing into as many structures as we could without arousing suspicion. We also paid careful attention to the waistband of every adult we passed.

Except for the uniformed guards, not one person in the village had a gun.

We started to make our way toward the outskirts of the village when we saw Ford walking toward us in his guard's uniform. The jacket was a stiff dark gray fabric with large buttons that mirrored each

Shattered Night

other in two rows down the center, only slightly different than the one from the man on the poster. I wondered if the differences meant his rank was higher. He looked pleasant enough, like he just wanted to say hello, until he heard the tone in Jordyn's voice. "Ford, what the hell?" Jordyn said. "How come none of these people have weapons of any kind? No guns? The only knife I saw could barely cut butter."

Within a second, Ford threw his hand over Jordyn's mouth and dragged her behind the closest building. Of course, we followed. "Damnit, Jordyn! You're going to get yourself thrown into a cell! You never could keep your mouth shut." I had never heard him speak to anyone like that, let alone someone I knew he respected.

I gently pried his hand off her mouth, and Olivia pulled her away from him. "Ford, what's going on? Do you mean to tell me the only people in this place who have means to protect themselves are the guards? And why would speaking her mind get her thrown in jail? This is still America, isn't it?"

Ford took a deep breath, seemed to consider his response for a moment, then nodded. "General Cole doesn't believe that there's a need for individual protection. His guards are a well-oiled machine. Many of them are former military, and even though they haven't seen combat they are very well-trained. There are also some who used to be Task Force officers. Guns or knives in the hands of the villagers would just cause chaos, especially since the village itself is getting overcrowded." He gestured to two little boys running by, playing with a soccer ball, nearly running into several people as they did. "Weapons caused the old America tons of problems. They will be able to grow up without fear of school shootings, robberies at gunpoint...they will grow up feeling secure. He says the crime rate here is nearly nonexistent."

My stomach lurched at his words. I debated on whether I should tell him who Cole really was, to help save him from himself, but the declaration lingered on my tongue unspoken. I just couldn't make the words come out until I knew it wouldn't mean the end for the rest of us. I trusted Ford, but Ford trusted Keegan...and that was a problem. The new information also made me realize that if some were former Task Force that meant there were other people around who knew who Keegan really was and didn't care. That fact was frightening enough on its own. "You don't find that strange at all? You buy this whole 'peace and harmony' thing?"

"Why wouldn't I?" He gestured toward the gun at his hip and looked into my eyes. "I can protect you Riley...all of you."

"I'd prefer to protect myself, thank you very much. I can't believe you're buying into this garbage, Ford," Jordyn said as she folded her arms across her chest like a disapproving mother.

Before Ford could respond, Olivia piped in. "Where's Reagan? Wasn't he supposed to be with you?"

"I had to go on patrol so he's in visiting Cain."

"Oh, okay...as thoroughly interesting as it is to watch you all argue, I think I'm going to go do that too. I'll see you later." Before I could stop her, she was marching back toward the house. Evidently, she had lost interest in trying to figure out our current circumstances.

"That was odd."

Jordyn snickered. "I'll explain it to you later but right now, let's focus on Moron Number One here. Ford, where do they keep the guns in this place?"

"In the armory under the jailhouse. Why?" The words had barely formed when he already knew the answer. "Jordyn, no. Forget it. There's no need for it anyway. Look around you. These people are happy here. No one here has any reason to complain. Everyone here has built a nice little life for themselves, and they won't have you screwing it up. The only thing you're going to get if you try to break in is your own private room in the jail. Seriously, forget it." There was an assuredness in his eyes, one that I had never seen before. Or maybe I had just never looked hard enough.

"He's right, Jordyn. It's too soon anyway. I know you want your gun back, but you know Cain's going to need a lot more medical care, and until he's better we are going to have to make nice. None of us can afford to piss anyone off right now. Let's go around and talk to some of the villagers, see who's who. Maybe, God forbid, make some friends."

Jordyn scoffed but Ford would hear none of it. "Listen to her, Jordyn."

"Fine. We'll go make friends. Get back to doing your bitch work." She waved him off with her hand like he was a fly buzzing around her, and didn't bother to hide the disgust in her face. "Shoo…"

With a deep sigh, Ford left. Jordyn faced me, arms still folded in a non-negotiating stance. "Can you believe that? He's really buying all this crap. It's like he's completely lost his mind. I hope he goes to fetch it soon."

I nodded. "Of course not, but for now, my first concern is getting Cain better..." I looked at her with assurance. "...and I know that's your goal too. The best thing we can do now is to gather as much information as we can about what we are dealing with. And from the looks of what we've found out so far, it's not good. These people are like...little fish swimming around in a bowl just waiting for someone to throw a hook in the water."

Jordyn stared at the town behind us. "There's one thing he's right about though."

"What's that?"

"These people have no reason to rock the boat, which means we are going to have to find them one and fast."

We took another lap around the village, looking for anyone who carried themselves in a way that suggested they'd be able to tell us about daily life in the village, but wouldn't go running their mouth about us asking. I paid careful attention to all the faces walking by, noticing if they were vigilant enough to even take a second glance at us. We were the newbies, so anyone who was paying attention should have been paying attention to *us*. "What was that about with Olivia? What did I miss?"

"Oh, honey, you haven't noticed her staring at Reagan when she thinks no one's watching?" she snickered. "You're getting rusty on me. Only a short time out of the compound and you're losing your touch. I do believe our Olivia has a crush."

I couldn't believe I hadn't picked up on it. "Really? God, you're right. I must be losing my edge."

Jordyn's face grew serious. She gently put her hand on my shoulder. "Well, it's not like you haven't had a lot of other stuff on your plate. Like the man you love almost dying, for one…oh, and figuring out that we are trapped in a town with his worst enemy at the head of the table. I can't imagine how horrible it would be to see Micah lying in a hospital bed like that."

I laughed, in a how-can-it-get-any-worse sort of way. "Yeah, there's that." My smile faded as soon as it came. "Seriously, what are we going to do? I can't deal with him lying there, at Keegan's mercy. My insides are in knots constantly."

She looked past my shoulder. "Well, for one, we're going to follow that guy over there who's been staring at us for the last two minutes."

I glanced behind me for just long enough to notice him nodding his head, motioning us over to him. His short-sleeved shirt was ragged and worn but looked fairly clean; much cleaner than his fingers which were caked with dirt under the nails. He struck me as a hard labor kind of man, not the kind that may have been an off-duty patrol guard.

"You sure?"

"Not at all, but at this point, not thinkin' we have many better options." A mischievous grin spread across her face. "And besides, if he tries anything, a good ass-kicking might be just what you need to get back on your game." She winked at me, and I couldn't help but smile.

A good ass-kicking did sound pretty nice.

CHAPTER TWO

Riley

We followed the stranger toward a small, off-white structure near the center of town, careful enough to keep our distance so that no one saw us together. It was bigger than the other tents but made of the same material, shaped like a large rectangle. We let him enter first, waiting a couple of minutes before going in ourselves. Once we were inside, my mind flooded with memories of the compound garden. The tent was packed tightly with plants of every size and color, bearing every type of fruit and vegetable I could think of, and a small potting bench made of wood the color of bright sand sat along the back wall.

"Come this way." I heard a voice through the foliage. We made our way through the trees, heavy with oranges and lemons, and the small blueberry bushes at our feet, careful not to step on the tender fruit. The man was standing next to the potting bench, almost invisible to us until we were upon him.

"I saw you looking around this morning. I know you're new; I know everyone around here. We haven't got anyone new in here in a while, probably because we're so crowded as it is. I'm surprised they let a group your size in at all." His words mirrored my thoughts earlier; he was actually aware of his surroundings, not complacent like the rest of the village. He paused for a moment, appearing to listen to the noises of people going about their days outside, and once he was satisfied that he didn't hear anything suspicious, he continued. "I saw you talking to that officer too. Correct me if I'm wrong, but it looked like you knew him…and weren't too happy about whatever he was saying."

I took a quick glance at Jordyn before responding. She nodded her permission for me to continue. "That's right, but how about we slow down a second. Who are you?"

He talked in a loud whisper as if the plants could hear him. "I'm Adam." He stuck his hand out.

I let my hand hover over his for a moment then took his in my own. "Riley. And this is Jordyn."

He nodded a greeting in her direction. "Glad to meet you both."

"So what's the story here? Why doesn't anyone have weapons?" Jordyn never did have time for pleasantries.

"I'll get to that. Things are…different here. It is good to meet people who think the same way we do."

"Who's we?" Jordyn asked.

He rubbed his dirty hand across his beard

stubble. "Most of the people here are happy. I've got to warn you. And they have every right to be. They have a place to live, food to eat, and *think* they are safe."

"What do you mean?'

He wiped his hands with a rag that was sitting on the potting bench. "I mean exactly that. They feel safe because there are big guys with guns around to supposedly protect them. But there are some of us around here who wonder what's going to happen if those people decide they don't want to protect us anymore, or that they want things done around here a certain way, maybe one that we aren't agreeable to." He turned to Jordyn. "I heard you ask the all-important question earlier today too—where are all the weapons? Well, they're not with the citizens of this village, that's for sure. The only weapons we have are anything heavy lying around our homes, and that's no match for a gun."

"So all these people are helpless without Kee—General Cole and his guys. Lovely," I said.

"Exactly."

"So how many of you are there?" Jordyn asked.

Adam hesitated. "Not a lot, I'll be honest. We've noticed a pattern where anybody who voices an opinion against the establishment here tends to disappear or die under suspicious circumstances. There have even been a few public hangings of people who of course were gagged so they couldn't tell anyone the real story before they found their feet in the air. So much for the First Amendment. I guess that part of America died with the government. We're told there are trials, but they are closed to the public. For all we know, the supposed criminals just sit there and the judge slams down his gavel because they have *guilty* eyes." He paused. "I haven't seen my brother in six months. Supposedly, he went on a supply run and disappeared." Adam struggled to finish. "He wouldn't do that. He wouldn't leave his wife and son behind. Or me. Something happened to him and I may never know what."

"People really put up with public hangings? That's barbaric."

Adam shrugged, an apologetic expression on his face as if he were responsible for the behavior of the masses. "I guess most people figure that if it's not someone they know they won't disrupt the status quo. I guess not everything has changed after all." He sighed. "What few of us there are, move carefully and talk to each other in secret."

"So how many?" I repeated Jordyn's question.

"Eight."

"Eight! Seriously? That's not much of a resistance." Jordyn quickly placed her hand to her forehead as if the small number had given her an instant headache. I didn't feel any better about it.

"But now you're here. And I can tell from how you acted today that you have some sort of training."

"Training?" I asked.

"Well, at least she," he pointed at Jordyn, "knew I was following you the entire time you were out there. That says to me that you've been trained by someone who knows what they're doing. I'm former military, so if you can catch me, you can catch anybody."

I turned to Jordyn. "Is that true? You only pointed him out a second ago. Why didn't you tell me?"

"So what do we do now?" She said, ignoring my question.

"We wait. The guards are going to be all over you for a while since you're new. They don't know what to make of you. So blend in, be normal, and when they've decided you aren't a threat, we'll figure out what to do next."

"One of our group is in the hospital. Blood poisoning. We can't do anything until he's well enough," I told him.

"That's ok. Trust me, it's going to take them a while to stop paying attention. They may be Cole's minions, but they aren't stupid. Just be sure to keep a close eye on your guard friend. He seems to have bought into all of this along with everyone else."

"Thank you, Adam. We will. And you watch your back too." I gave him a pleasant smile. It was a relief to have allies inside the village, no matter how few.

He picked up a small plant that had been sitting on his potting bench. "You both be careful." He smiled. "I'm going to go back to gardening. Somebody's got to feed this place. And never underestimate the value of a good distraction."

Once we were outside, I grabbed Jordyn by the arm. "Why didn't you tell me that he was following us?"

Jordyn yanked herself free. "For God's sake, Riley. Missing Olivia's infatuation with Reagan was one thing, but Jesus...you are supposed to be good at this. I shouldn't have to tell you anything. And the fact that you are even asking me that quite honestly freaks me out." She grabbed me by the shoulders and looked at me square in the eyes. "I know you're worried about Cain, but he wouldn't put up with this and neither will I. Get your shit together. Seriously. You're worrying me. We need to be more on our game than ever and every time I turn around you're gazing up into the clouds." She turned around and marched back toward our housing, leaving me to stand by myself with the dust swirling around my feet.

Not feeling very social after that, I used the time to walk to the edge of the village. There was a stream running through it, and I hoped the sound of the rushing water would help me clear my head. I stared down into the rippling surface, realizing that I already had the clarity I needed; I just didn't want to admit it. Jordyn was right. I was being sloppy. Without Cain by my side, I was a flag twisting in the brewing storm. I had made it without him for years, but now that I had him, functioning without him seemed impossible.

And knowing that he was lying in a hospital bed unable to defend himself was more than I could stand. I imagined Keegan hovering over him, a sadistic smile spread across his face, waving a knife gingerly above his throat, ready to give Cain a wound that matched his own. Or maybe he would be subtler, sticking something toxic into his IV bag, and when Cain died Keegan would make a big show of firing whatever unfortunate doctor was on call that night. Maybe it wouldn't even be poison, just the wrong medicine at the wrong time, something that could easily be explained as an oversite by a staff member. Accidents happen, and I knew Keegan was capable of manufacturing a wider variety of them than I cared to think about.

Either way, we would know the truth and be helpless to stop it. The only thing we could do is guard him as much as possible and hope that he would heal before it was too late. So as I stared into the liquid flowing by me, carrying little bits of leafy debris, I made a promise to myself that Cain would never approve of. If Keegan decided to take Cain from me, if I came to his hospital room to find him gone forever, I would take Keegan from this world myself. Cain never wanted me to have blood on my hands for him, but if that were to happen, I knew that blood would be the only thing that would keep me from living the rest of my life in the empty abyss left by his absence. After losing Cain, a long life would be more of a curse than a gift.

Though Jordyn had been rather brutal, I tried to remember that she was going through something too. She had left her husband and stepdaughter behind to go to the village first with us, to help us make sure it was safe. Sure, she wanted to do it to protect her family, but that also meant leaving them behind. We left them at a secure location, but we were living in an unsafe world. She had just settled into a life with him when war found its way to our doorstep back at the compound, and now she found herself on the edge of a fight once again. She had to know that until we had our situation solved, there would be no reuniting with them. Time was not on our side, and it seemed that nothing else was either.

When I got back to our room, I thought it was empty at first, until I noticed my mother staring out our blinds-covered windows, her face a mix of shadows and light. The messy curls that I knew from the compound were now tied back in a well-kept ponytail, and her shirt was silky-looking, hanging gently over the top of her well-fitting jeans. She was the perfect mix of the two halves of herself: a polished public figure, and a worker who spent her days side-by-side with the people around her, hands in the dirt like everyone else. I threw my arms around her. "Thank God you're here! I thought you had lost your mind yesterday."

Her arms loosened. "Riley, I need to talk to you."

Something in her eyes made me cringe. "Why?"

"Just sit down, I don't have a lot of time." I followed her to Olivia's bed, which was the closest. "I know this may be hard for you to believe, but sometimes people change." Her expression was so formal, like a teacher scolding a student. The mother who was my best friend was somewhere else.

"Oh, no, you—"

"General Cole…Marcus has made a great life for himself here. And a great life for all these people. I'm sure you surveyed everything today. People are very happy here. It reminds them of what America used to be."

The way she called him by his first name made a sweat break out across my body. I had held out

Shattered Night

hope...a very slight bit, but a bit nonetheless, that she didn't know who he was. It was very possible for ordinary citizens not to recognize Keegan, but my mom had been in the government around the same time he was. The odds of her not figuring out his true identity were disappointingly slim. "Mom, you can't be serious. You know what he did to Cain."

She sighed. "Yes, and it was absolutely terrible. Unforgivable, in fact. But I'm not asking you to forgive him. I'm asking you to remember that we've all done things since the collapse that we aren't proud of. Me included. *Especially* me for goodness sakes. If we cut out everyone who has made a bad decision we'd have no one left."

I jolted off the bed as if she'd stabbed a needle through my skin. "A *bad decision*? He's a murderer!"

"So is Cain." She stared at me. I wouldn't have felt more pain from her words if she had stuck an ice pick through my chest.

"That's not the same. He killed those girls just because he could. To make Cain suffer."

"That may be true, but look at this place. It's not just a place for people to eat and sleep, it's a civilization. Don't you think it's possible that he's changed? Don't you think it's possible that he's different now?"

"They hang people here, Mom! *Hang* them! He still wants to hurt Cain. I know he does. Did you see the smile on his face when we got here? He just wants to play with us, to torture us with the knowledge that he could kill us at any time."

She tried to take my hands, but I pulled away. "Why wouldn't he have just killed Cain right away if he was going to hurt him? Why would he be providing him with medical care? Cain's here right now getting the best help from a doctor that he could possibly get for a thousand miles. And that's because of Marcus."

My voice rose. "He's doing it because he's enjoying this! Don't you see it? He has the upper hand and he knows it."

"Riley don't be ridiculous. He's got much more important things to worry about than Cain. You're being a little dramatic." The mother that had always taken me seriously, who had always respected my opinion, was now looking at me with vacant eyes as if I were a client she had to explain something unpleasant to and was growing impatient with me. Her condescension was thick, and I was finding myself unable to wade through it. Something was very wrong, and I had no idea how to fix it. And given the way she was behaving, I wasn't sure I wanted to.

A lump formed in my throat but I refused to let her see the tears that threatened to come. So like any self-respecting daughter, I yelled louder. "I can't believe you! You're just going to turn your back on Cain? On me? For *him*? How is this even possible?"

"No one is turning their back on anyone. Now—"

"Get out." I leaped off the bed.

"Riley—"

"You heard me. Get out!"

Shattered Night

"I—"

I never thought I would, but at that moment, I put my hands on my mother. I pulled her off the bed hard and shoved her out the door. "And don't come back. Ever. And stay away from Dominic. You're too stupid to see what's right in front of you. You don't deserve him."

As I slammed the door in her face, the tears came with a vengeance, in the form of spine-clenching, echoing screams.

CHAPTER THREE

Cain

I can't say I heard him before I saw his face; it was more like a change in the air. I had been waiting for him, knowing he would come, just not knowing when. Would he toy with me? Or would he grow impatient and kill me right then, knowing that the thing he had wanted for years, my death, was now in his grasp? I was pretty sure it would be the former, but many things had changed over the course of ten years. Perhaps he would be so anxious to do away with me that he wouldn't be able to savor it, and I would quickly find a knife at my throat. Or maybe he would prefer a gunshot to my head, letting me disappear into a fog of pink mist. Either way, I would be gone. "I knew you would come." In my head, my voice sounded strong, but it came out a rasping whisper, getting lost among the beeping monitors and the whispers of strangers in far-off rooms.

The door clicked shut behind him. "Of course. I

wouldn't miss the chance to see an old friend from the before-time, before everything imploded. There aren't many of us left, you know." The same smile from ten years ago greeted me once again, the one that appeared right before he tore my world apart. He always had the ability to go from pleasant servant of the people to sociopath with a lift of a brow, or a twitch in the corner of his mouth.

"I'm not your friend."

Keegan laughed. "Well, what would you call us then? We've been so wrapped up in each other—tangled in each other's lives—we couldn't really be called anything else. You are my life-changer, Cain Foley. My anchor. The one person that keeps me focused but always seems to weigh me down. You are the center of my five-pointed star, the place where all the spokes of my wheel bind together."

"I could think of a couple different things to call us." I grew rigid as he sat in the chair by my bed, the same chair that Riley, Dom, and everyone else I loved had been in over the last few days. Seeing him in the same space seemed so wrong, so tainted. The thought crossed my mind that if I shut my eyes tight and opened them again, the vision I wanted would be there in the nightmare's place. And, same as when I tried it as a child, it didn't work. "Will you kill me today? Or will you wait until tomorrow?" I swallowed, trying to calm the dryness in my throat. I wanted the answer, yet I still wished I hadn't asked the question. Maybe it was better to know, or maybe I wanted to live just a couple seconds longer thinking that I would see Riley just one more time. "Or maybe you haven't decided yet?

I am sure it's a big decision. Always best to weigh your options."

Keegan's eyes narrowed. "Oh, Cain. I could tell you that I have no intention of killing you. That I have forgiven you over the years. That all I want is to keep this new life I've built with Claire by my side, and hopefully you as well. I could spin you some line about wanting us to work together to build a better future, but surely we've known each other too long for that."

"I agree completely."

He leaned closer to me. "It's true, I have no intention of killing you, at least not today. Claire has yet to outgrow her usefulness, and I'm sure she would disapprove of me ending you. The people here adore her, and as you saw when you got here, she feels the same about me." He pointed to his own neck, running his finger across the square of skin where I had stuck a pair of surgical scissors years before. "There would be something poetic about us having matching scars though. But now is not the time. Besides, there are so many of your dear friends that I need to get acquainted with." He paused for a moment, running through the list in his head. "That Jordyn girl for one…never had the pleasure until now. Her reputation precedes her. Quite the gunslinger I've heard. Tell me, does she still sell herself for money? I'm sure she could charge quite a bit. So athletic…"

My jaw tightened. I tried to raise myself up on my forearms but fell right back toward my pillow, my body betraying my heart. "You stay away from her, you hear me?"

Shattered Night

Keegan leaned back in his chair, arms folded across his chest. "Oh, I hear you loud and clear, I'm just not going to abide by your rules…" He acted as though he just remembered something. "That's right! She has a lovely husband and daughter now. How nice. Too bad about her dead father though. Tragic really."

I tried again to rise from the bed, but my arms felt empty and my legs seemed hollow. Heat brewed all over my exhausted body. He was not supposed to know every detail of our lives back at the compound, and my mouth tasted of bile as I wondered how he had gotten that information.

"On a side note, you'll be happy to know that I've taken care of the vast list of bounties out on you. You seem to have annoyed quite a few people in the past ten years. Nevertheless, the world has been warned not to touch a hair on your knobby little head, or to capture you, and if they do, they will have to answer to me and my comrades. The outside world still knows me as Marcus Keegan, the man in line for the presidency, who survived as the rest of the government ran away or died." I stared at him. "Let's just say my reputation precedes me too. You're welcome."

"Saving me for yourself huh?"

He grinned menacingly. "Of course. Isn't that what we both deserve though? A death as epic as our time together? Do you really want to fall at the hands of some two-bit revolutionary who happened to get in a lucky shot? It would have been a pity if that idiot back on the compound had hit you slightly to the left."

I swallowed hard. "How did you know that? *Any* of that?"

He shook his head condescendingly. "Cain, oh Cain, I have eyes and ears everywhere. I was the head of the Task Force for God's sake. I've been watching you for years, just waiting for the right time. And that time is now."

If I'd had the strength, I would have spit fire. "The right time? You mean the time where I'm wounded and can't defend myself? Wow, Keegan, you never struck me as a man afraid of a fair fight. Then again, you did gun down a group of defenseless girls simply because one of them pissed you off."

His face reddened, and he slammed his fist against the side of the bed. "Pissed me off? I would say killing my brother goes way beyond the realm of leaving me 'pissed off.' And fair? Your gunshot wound was just an added bonus. You were already on your way here. And was it fair when you left me to die when you set my police station on fire? Was that fair then? An explosion from one of the morgue chemicals was the only thing that saved me, blasting a hole in the wall that became my way out. There was a heavy price to pay for my escape though." He lifted his shirt, and I could see now that on the side of his body he had a large scar of his own. "My wound got infected at some point as I dragged my broken body across the ground for help. I was laid up in a hospital for months. Red, bubbly-looking, ghastly thing it was. The bloated flesh of a corpse had nothing on me." I noticed the muscles in his face tighten. "I was quite a sight, much like you are now." He stared at me, eyes cutting into me like the blades I yearned to have back at my side.

"Now who else do I want to get acquainted with? Yes, that little redhead too, now she's a beauty. Takes after her mother. That gorgeous hair, that soft little angel face…I intend on getting to know her intimately." He leaned so uncomfortably close that I could feel his breath on my face. His voice hissed, "Don't you worry, I'll take real good care of her. I'll make sure I give her everything she needs. By the time I'm done with her, she won't want you anymore at all."

My entire body grew hotter than I knew was possible. Anger swelled inside me and I felt I may burst at the seams. Something deep in my very center gave me the strength to launch myself toward him. But as quickly as I felt myself fly through the air, I landed hard on the white linoleum floor below, taking a heap of wires and IV bags with me. A wave of new pain washed over me as the monitors started buzzing, and I looked over to see little streams of blood seeping out of both my arms where the IV needles had ripped out.

Keegan clapped his hands together in gleeful triumph. "It *is* her. I suspected as much. It was either Jordyn…I do love a good extramarital affair…or her. The way she looked at you, I could tell how she felt, but that's so sweet that you feel the same. It's just dripping off of you. Love can be such a perfect, unbreakable thing, don't you think?"

I was in too much pain to respond, suspicious that my mind hurt as much as my muscles, knowing that I'd given away the most precious secret I had.

The doctor arrived quickly, but Keegan had enough time to get himself to the other side of the room. "General, what happened?"

"I'm not sure, Doctor. I had just come in as he fell to the floor." Keegan watched as a nurse swiftly glided in after the doctor. As they carefully picked me up off the floor and laid me back in bed, fixing the tubes and the needles once I was safely there, he stared at me, smiling. "Thank you, Doctor. Be sure to give him extra attention. He's not taking kindly to being out of commission."

"Yes, Sir."

Keegan gave me a wink then shut the door behind him. Talking to him one-on-one again was somewhat freeing, when that moment that you anticipate for years and know is inevitable finally comes to pass. But that freedom was overshadowed by the pure fear I held deep in my heart, knowing I had given away my biggest vulnerability: I was in love.

Not long after Keegan left, Riley burst into the room. Her wild red hair flew behind her, and despite everything Keegan had said, it made me smile. She had a way of making me forget the chaos and be unable to see anything but her.

But this time, it was only for a moment.

"Cain! What happened? You look worse off than you did last time I was in here." She slid over to me in the chair and grabbed my hand. "It was him, wasn't it? What has he done to you? How'd he even get in here? Someone is supposed to be with you every minute and—"

"Riley, you have to listen to me. I messed up."

Shattered Night

"What do you mean?"

I paused, afraid if I said the words out loud that would make them real. But I knew I had to warn her and couldn't wait a moment longer. "He hit a nerve and I messed up. He figured out that it's you; you're the one I'm in love with. He started baiting me with Jordyn, then he got to you, and I just snapped. That's how I ended up on the floor. You're in more danger now than you were before, and that's my fault." I turned away from her, unable to look at the face that had captivated me since she had walked into my hideout as a fearless teenager.

She sighed, as if in relief, which made me even more terrified than I had been before. "It's okay. You know I can take care of myself. My mother seems to be fairly high up in this place after all. He wouldn't do anything to me that I can't handle. We just need you to get better as soon as possible. We found out some information about—"

"I am going to talk to Dom and have him get you out of here. He can sneak you out tonight. I'm sure Ford would help. You have to leave and not look back. I promise I will find you."

Riley jumped back. "No way. You know that's not going to happen."

"Please, Riley, I'm begging you. I can't lose you."

She leaned over and gently kissed me on the forehead. "Shut it. I'm not going anywhere. We're going to need both of us to beat these people. Don't you think even if I run away, he could find me? If he got rid of me out there, he could hide what he did from my mother and keep her at his side. My best bet is to stay here. He can't hurt me if he wants to have anything to do with my mother."

I thought back to what Keegan said, about having eyes and ears everywhere, and realized she was right. As much as it made me feel more desperate and panicked than anything ever had before, I knew it was true.

"I'm safer here where we can all keep an eye on him, where we all have each other, than out there. And I think there's even more going on here than we thought. This is much bigger than a power-hungry man feeding his own ego."

"What did you see?"

Her voice hushed into a whisper. "It's more like what we didn't see. Cain, no one here has any weapons. The guards took all of them and locked them away somewhere. These people are completely defenseless."

Sounds about right, I thought. "Are the people outraged?"

"That's the thing. They're happy. They're too happy to realize how much danger they are in. Except for Adam and his friends."

My jaw tightened. After everything we'd been through, new people made me nervous. "Who is Adam?"

"There are a few people who can see the position they are in. But they are small in number. Really small. And I have no idea if they can fight."

I smiled mischievously, though my confidence was more for show than I wanted to admit. "All they need is the desire. I can teach them the rest." I used the remaining strength that I had to kiss her hand. "And so can you."

"I love you so much."

The love in her eyes made my heart swell with happiness and ache all at the same time, and giving into my own guilt, I let myself wonder how much easier her life would be if she had never met me.

"I love you too, Riley. Tell Jordyn to watch her back too. He made it clear that he has his eye on everyone I love, but especially you two. Thank God Micah and McKenzie aren't here. He mentioned them specifically."

Her face grew pale. "Oh my God, he's a monster."

"Yes, he is. But we're going to beat him, somehow. We have no choice. He can't carry on this façade forever, and when his veneer breaks, we, and all these innocent people will pay the price. Find out as much as you can about where the weapons are kept. Ford will tell you, but don't let him in on why. We can't be sure we can trust him."

She looked away from me, and I could tell there was something she didn't want to say. "What is it?"

"We can't trust my mother either while we're at it."

I stared at her, waiting for her to finish. When she didn't, I said, "He's gotten into her head too, hasn't he? I was hoping what I saw when we first got here was just my fevered brain playing tricks on me."

"Yes. I had hoped that she was being held against her will, but she's not. Cain, it was awful. She was just spewing garbage about how he's changed and how he's a new man and doing all these amazing things. I kicked her out of my room…out of our lives."

"Riley…"

She shook her head. "No, it's done with. She betrayed you…she betrayed both of us. I won't have it."

"She's still your mother and she would do anything for you, you know that."

She glared, more at her mother than at me. "Yeah, except the one thing I need the most…I need her to trust me."

"I promise you, Keegan will make a mistake. That's all that needs to happen…he will make a mistake, and when he does, your mom will see it. She may be naïve but she's not stupid. You'll see." I hoped I was right. I had to believe I was right. She didn't deserve to lose her mother, and I knew if she did that I was partially responsible. She'd paid too much for loving me already.

She scoffed. "Well let's hope he makes a mistake soon because until then, I want nothing to do with her."

"You and she are closer than any mother and daughter I've ever seen. Don't give up on her. Not yet…promise me?"

She hesitated for a moment then nodded. "All right. I'll try." She got up and headed toward the door, then ran back and kissed me passionately on the mouth. "I love you." Her chin trembled.

"What is it?"

"I can't help but be terrified every time I leave this room that it will be the last time I see you. Cain, I'm so scared."

I smiled at her. "Loving you already got me out of this bed once. It will do it again. I'll be back to who I once was before you know it. Just have faith, please? Everything is going to be all right."

"How do you know?"

"Because God doesn't let the devil win. Dom taught me that a long time ago. And Keegan...even if he isn't the devil himself, he's damn close. We're going to be ok, I promise you. We will find a way to beat him."

She gently stroked my cheek with her hand. "Ok. I love you. Please get better soon."

When the door shut behind her, I admitted something to myself that I wouldn't admit to her. Every time she left, I felt the same fear and prayed Keegan wouldn't take her away from me before I saw her again. My faith in God had always carried me through, but I had lived enough to know that God's plan and mine were not always the same.

CHAPTER FOUR

Keegan

I settled down in the chair in my room, which overlooked the village. I crossed my legs comfortably and let out a victorious sigh. It had happened. The moment I had waited to happen for years had finally come to pass. But as I pretended to look at a book I had grabbed from the shelf next to the chair, I didn't feel the elation that I had expected. This was my after, or at the very least, my present that would eventually morph into a finality I wasn't sure I was prepared for: I had won. The man who had taken my brother away from me was finally under my control, lying in a hospital bed unable to dress himself, let alone fight. Yes, he wasn't directly responsible for his death, but it didn't matter. The second he joined up with the woman who *had* been, he lined himself up for execution. His punishment would be long, more mental than physical, and the climax would be when I snuffed out his life.

Shattered Night

But what would happen after?

What did the universe look like without Cain Foley in it? I hadn't known one such as that for a very long time. I'd acquired power beyond any I had ever imagined back when the two of us had first met. And when I had my way, I would rise even further very soon, and no one would know it was coming.

It didn't have to turn out this way, not really. Cain had every opportunity to tell me what I'd needed to know, but he didn't. Instead, he decided to help cover up a crime. He robbed me of any chance I had to put my own brother to rest, and now he would experience firsthand what it was like to see the people closest to you slowly unravel before your eyes. That's what he deserved, and that's what I would deliver.

The village below me was alive. I made a point of watching them at the same time every day, watching as their routines changed or stayed the same. Part of it was to relish in what I'd accomplished, and the other was to be the omnipresent leader that the people below me so desperately needed. I noticed they avoided looking at my window, moving about their day as if they all had somewhere critical that they needed to be. That was ok. People tended to behave more like their authentic selves when they could pretend no one was watching.

I was always watching.

The population of the village was at capacity. Every day, it was more evident as I gazed out at the people, free space slowly being suffocated. I pretended to be distraught about our population problem. But what no one knew, was that I'd wanted it that way.

It was a perfectly reasonable excuse for what would happen next.

I got up from my chair and poured myself a glass of bourbon from the bottle I kept hidden under my t-shirts. Perhaps I'd visit Cain again, and bring him one. He'd assume I'd put poison in it, and I could grin as I drank his share of perfectly delicious alcohol. It'd probably been years, if ever, since he'd had anything decent to drink.

I poured him a glass anyway, one that he would never have. I clinked my glass against his, raising mine in a toast to no one in particular. Perhaps I was toasting to where we had been, two members of an era long dead, from a life no one lived in anymore.

What was my after?

Cain was my reflection, not different, yet not the same. And when I was done with him, the creature that looked back at me would be a million miles away from the hurricane he once was. For a storm such as his to destroy everything in its path, it needs power. When you take away that, a cyclone becomes a morning breeze.

When I was finished, he would be nothing more than a whisper.

CHAPTER FIVE

Riley

Jordyn and Olivia were both in our room when I got there. I closed the door carefully behind me and slid a chair that we had in the corner under the knob for good measure. "What's going on?" Olivia asked.

"Keegan said something to Cain that made him try to get out of bed and he ended up on the floor." I turned to Jordyn. "He told me to tell you to watch out. Keegan mentioned me and you specifically when he was trying to scare him."

"If he wound up on the floor, obviously it worked," Jordyn said. She sighed as she glanced up from the book she was reading. "Of course I can't blame him. Is anyone with him now?"

"Reagan is." Olivia stared at the door as she said his name. "He went back after we talked for a while."

Glad to find a momentary distraction from our situation, I smirked. "Oh yeah? You were awfully excited to find him earlier today."

Olivia scowled at me. "Before you start making too much fun of me, would you like to hear everything there is to know about the armory or not?"

Jordyn and I sat eagerly on the bed, waiting for her reply. Olivia may not know how to fight, but she was clever, and ever since we found her back in Rome, that survival skill seemed to come in handy just as much as our knife-skills had.

Before she could begin though, there was a knock at our door. I moved the chair and suspiciously opened the door a crack, afraid I would see Keegan's menacing face on the other side. Relief flooded me when I saw Nick and Dom instead. "You guys are just in time. Olivia was about to tell us about the armory."

"Hell yes. Gettin' armed sounds pretty good right about now," Nick said. As long as I've known him, he was always ready for a fight, and the years and the proximity to Cain's worst enemy hadn't changed that. He looked as though he would continue, but Dom gave him a fatherly time-to-be-quiet look so he sat down with his hands folded neatly in his lap.

According to what Ford told Reagan, there was more than one armory, and the main one was in the basement of the very place we were sitting, not the jail as he had said before. That was where they housed a small number of weapons, but, of course, there were other places spread around the village just in case. Keegan—or General Cole as Ford still referred to him—was too smart to keep all his weaponry in one spot. I wasn't sure if Ford just thought of both places as armories, or if he withheld some of the truth before to protect us.

Ford also said that the General only let a few trusted individuals down there, and Ford was lucky enough to be one of them. The only place he was not allowed to go to was a large warehouse-looking place at the edge of the village. There were several other warehouses in the area. Some were used for food storage, and some for emergency housing. But there was only the one that Keegan kept guarded twenty-four hours a day. Reagan was very curious about it, but Ford said not to concern himself with it, for risk of him getting in trouble. Apparently, everyone was aware that building was off limits, and to contradict that meant a day in a cell, if not more. That was where Ford was now, taking a shift at the jail.

"So obviously, we have to figure out a way into that warehouse. Probably before the armory so we know what we're dealing with," Dom stated.

"You're right. Once we get our weapons back all hell is going to break loose." As Nick spoke, a realization occurred to me. I ran over to the air vent in the wall, and unscrewed it. Carefully, I removed Cain's knives from their hiding spot. "Nick, Keegan knows about me and Cain. Eventually, he's going to go through my stuff." I handed the knives to him. "I think these are safer with you."

He nodded. "I'll guard these with my life, you know that."

I smiled and squeezed him on the shoulder. "Please, don't go that far."

Jordyn looked at me. "Where's your knife, Riley?"

"During the day, in my mattress. At night, under my pillow where it belongs."

Nick threw his hand back out. "Hand it over. You know he'll find it."

My smile disappeared as I reluctantly reached under the mattress, right next to where Nick was sitting. "Take good care of it."

"Of course I will."

The group of us knew that in order to eat, we had to go to the kitchen downstairs where Keegan, his guards, and the doctors all ate. The villagers all cooked in their respective homes, but for us, we didn't have a home. On top of that if we dared pass on the chance to eat with the great General Cole all eyes would be upon us, something that we could not afford. Keeping up appearances was crucial.

So, fighting every ounce of instinct we had, we marched downstairs and sat at one of the thin, plastic foldout tables in the small cafeteria room. When we arrived, I saw my mother sitting beside Keegan, along with two guards I didn't recognize, and the doctor who was treating Cain. There was one nurse already seated at the table we chose—a round, jolly woman with a dirty apron who smiled brightly as we entered, excitedly tapping her fingers, apparently thrilled to have company. "Hello! Welcome. I haven't seen you around here before. When did you arrive?"

I smiled back at her and was about to answer when the voice I despised more than anything in the world rang out behind me. "Riley, why don't you

Shattered Night

all come sit down over here with us? There's plenty of room at this giant table. Feel free to bring your new friend." The nurse's eyes brightened, and I could tell this was the first time she had been *honored* by being asked to join the general. She sat up straighter and got up from the table before any of the rest of us moved an inch and ran her hands down her apron in an attempt to smooth out the wrinkles. I bit the inside of my cheek to keep from grimacing at the suggestion but knew that we didn't have a choice. With a sigh, we all gave knowing glances to one another and took our meals over to the other table.

I sat as far away from my mother as I could. As I stared into my vegetables, hoping they weren't laced with something, out of the corner of my eye, I caught her looking at me several times. "So, Riley, how are you liking it here so far?" Keegan asked.

Taking a deep breath, I answered him. "It's great."

"Great? Just great? What about it have you enjoyed the most?

He was not about to let me off that easy. Dom tried to save me. "We've all loved our new accommodations, General. It's good to all be under one roof."

"Glad to hear it, Father. Riley, have you explored the town?"

"Yes, we all have. It's…great."

Keegan laughed. "*Great* again. You seem very fond of that word, dear. Claire, has she always been so talkative?"

My mother's cheeks flushed. "Sorry, she just

needs a little time to get adjusted."

I slammed my fork down on the table. Not only was my mother sleeping with the enemy (possibly literally and figuratively), she was now apologizing for me? Not ok. But…in the midst of my anger grew an idea. I put on the politest smile I could muster. "No need to apologize, Mom. I guess I just haven't had the whole experience yet. If it's not too much trouble, General, would you mind giving me a personal tour tomorrow? I'm sure seeing it through your eyes would give me an even wider perspective. I'd love to get your take on all of this." As soon as I said it, I could feel Jordyn, Olivia, Dom, and Nick's eyes on me, staring at me with both disbelief and fear.

Keegan smiled. "Of course. It would be my pleasure." He put his arm around my mother and kissed her on the cheek. I hope he didn't see me cringe. "I always have time for Claire's daughter. I'll come knocking on your door first thing tomorrow. Perhaps your mother can join us."

I forced a smile. "I was thinking it could just be you and I if that's ok. I'm sure Mom has seen the town countless times. Besides, since it's obvious you two have grown close, I would love the chance to get to know you better." Maybe, just maybe, I could convince him that Cain hadn't told me what he had done, and I was coming into the situation with a clean slate. I ignored the disappointment in my mother's eyes.

"Whatever you want, Riley. I'd be happy to. I'm rather proud of what we've done here."

"Fantastic. Looking forward to it." It was a risk,

Shattered Night

yes, but one worth taking. If I could get Keegan to think that I didn't know what he did to Cain, that I only knew him as General Cole, maybe I could figure out a piece of information that would help us get out of that place, and save these people from what would eventually mold into a dictatorship at the very best or who knows what else at the very worst.

The rest of dinner went by slower than any of us would have liked. We all stared down into our Salisbury steak as if the reddish muscle tissue could tell us what came next. I could feel our group wanting to drag me upstairs and ask me what the hell I was thinking, which I was sure I was in for once we got back to our rooms. But I used the time to talk to Cain's doctor, and see how his progress was coming along.

"He's doing fairly well. I briefed my colleague on his progress, and I'll introduce you next time you're visiting. He will be taking over in a few weeks when I leave."

"Leave? But why would you leave? I mean, it's so nice here…"

When the doctor told me he'd be transferring Cain's case, I noticed Keegan set his hand down on the table with a bit more force than necessary. "We have built some relationships with other villages. There's one nearby who unfortunately does not have a doctor. Since we have two, Doctor Borden and his family will be moving there, freeing up a little space in our overcrowded town, and helping out our neighbors in the process."

As I glanced back and forth between Keegan and

the doctor, I realized something was very wrong. Keegan would never give up a valuable resource unless there was something in it for him. While Keegan spoke, Dom and I exchanged a confused look, and I could tell he was wondering the same thing. There was more to this move than philanthropy. "Anyway, no need to worry. Cain will be in good hands, I promise. After his fall today, his body is a little banged up, but he seems to be taking nicely to the fluids and the cleansing of his blood. He's strong, so he should come along smoothly. As long as he listens and stays in bed like I am telling him to do."

"A fall? I thought he'd looked worse off, but Cain told me it was my imagination. What happened?" I caught Keegan looking at me, but figured Cain downplaying an injury was plausible, especially if he was trying to keep who Keegan really was a secret.

"He must have rolled out of bed on accident. Happens every once in a while—someone has a bad dream and is trying to escape in their sleep and ends up on the floor." The doctor placed his fork on his tray and started to get up. "If it happens again, we may have to install some guard rails on his bed. Do you know if he has a history of nightmares?"

I sighed. "You have no idea."

As soon as we were safely back up in our room, Dom, Nick, Olivia, and Jordyn all laid into me at once. "What were you thinking?"

I don't want you alone with him.
This is way too dangerous.
Don't be an idiot. Fake sick or something.

Shattered Night

I held out my hands in an attempt to silence them. "I'll be fine I promise. I couldn't pass up the opportunity. Besides, we will be walking through town, so I won't be alone. If I can learn something, anything that might help us, it's worth it, you have to admit that. Maybe I can even convince him that I'm not totally repulsed by him, and he may open up to me. I'm sure he'd love to torture Cain by having some sort of pretend friendship with me."

Silence.

Nick was the first to speak. "I know you're right, but I don't have to like it."

"You're right, you don't," I said warmly. "I promise I'll be ok you guys."

"I have to tell Cain. He's going to be pissed." Nick folded his arms across his chest, like a small child when they're itching to tattle on someone. But coming from him, it was charming.

"Maybe, but hopefully I'll be able to share some new information that will soften the blow. And at least don't tell him until after I've already left. If you give him a chance to try and stop me he'll probably try to get out of bed and hurt himself even more. That's the last thing we need."

I sat down on the bed as Reagan came into the room. He had taken some food to Ford on his shift and looked as if for some reason he hadn't expected all of us to be there at once. "Oh, hey guys. Olivia, you ready?"

She smiled at him. "Absolutely. Let's go."

Nick asked what we all wanted to. "Where are you going? Are you going on a date or something?"

Reagan's cheeks turned red. "Something like

that. Unfortunately, there aren't any fancy restaurants around here. All I can really do is take her out to watch the stars."

"Awwwwww…." Jordyn said. "Cuuuuuuute."

"Yes, she is," Reagan said with a mischievous smile, evidently knowing full well that's not what she meant.

Olivia winked at us as they walked out the door arm in arm. In the midst of everything that was going on, it was nice to see two people find a way to grow something special among the madness. God knows Olivia deserved some happiness.

After Dom and Nick went to bed, Jordyn and I decided to crawl into one bed, like most sisters do when the world seems dark. We never could back at the compound since our beds were so small, so that was one light spot in our captivity. As we pulled the silky white covers over us, she said, "You be damn careful tomorrow, ok?"

"Of course I will."

"Seriously, Riley, I mean it. You're sloppy right now and this is not the time to be sloppy. He's a shark and you get no second chances."

I smiled. "Is that your way of saying you love me? Tell me you *love* me…"

"Shut up and promise me." She tried to hold in a smile, but I could see it trying to peek out of the edges of her mouth.

As quickly as the conversation started, silence overtook us. Jordyn was the first to speak. "Tell me Cain's going to be ok. I hate leaving him in there."

"Me too. Keegan got to him today. Even with one of us guarding him constantly, Keegan can still force them out of the room. He's in charge and there's nothing we can do about it."

"At least not yet. Maybe after tomorrow that will be different."

"Exactly."

Silence fell upon us once again. I listened to the sounds of the night playing in the air, and I wondered if the people would ever understand how much danger they were in. From the music and laughter drifting up to us, my guess was no, and maybe that was ok. Maybe we could save them before they would have to find out, and no one else would have to die.

"Micah loved that song," Jordyn said suddenly.

"Which one?"

"Hear that flute? He used to sing that same tune to McKenzie when he put her down for her nap. Worked every time. He never said what it was, but I'd recognize it anywhere." She smiled. "I've never told anyone this, but sometimes, when I couldn't sleep, he'd sing it to me too. Kind of ruins my image, you know?"

I gave her a good-natured nudge. "Your secret is safe with me, don't worry. I won't tell anyone my gun-toting sister likes lullabies."

She poked me in the ribs. "You better not."

As I drifted off into a fitful sleep, I prayed that by that time tomorrow, I would have something that might help me save us all.

***

Keegan arrived the next morning while we were

getting dressed. He opened the door to find me, Jordyn and Olivia all in our bras and underwear. Instinctively, we threw our hands and arms across our bodies, attempting to block ourselves as much as we could. "Oh, gosh, I apologize. I should have knocked."

"Damn right you should have," Olivia said. Though I agreed, I hoped her attitude was not about to get her thrown in jail.

As he apologized again, he took his time leaving the room, lingering in the open doorway. Though he was sly about it, I felt his eyes move up and down all of us, taking in every inch of the free peep show he'd given himself. His smooth, underworked hand gripped the doorknob. "I'll be outside when you're ready."

When he finally shut the door, the three of us collectively shivered. "Riley, this is a bad idea," Olivia whispered so Keegan couldn't hear. "Please don't do this. At least let one of us go with you." The concerned expression on her face almost made me agree. I didn't want to do it in the first place, especially after that latest violation. But we needed whatever ammunition the day would bring us, and I was in the position to get it. I couldn't give that up.

"It's definitely not something I'm looking forward to, that's for damn sure." I went over to her and gave her a hug. "I can't have one of you with me because there's no chance he'll open up that way and the whole thing will be a waste. It'll be ok though, I promise. If I'm not back by tonight come looking for me ok?" Both she and Jordyn reluctantly nodded. "It'll be worth it. This whole

Shattered Night

day will be worth it."

Jordyn and Olivia put their arms around each other, perhaps to keep one another from falling on the floor under the weight of what I was about to do. As I hovered my hand above the doorknob, not sure that I was ready to meet what was on the other side, I looked back at one girl who had been there for me for years, and the other that I had finally seemed to have broken through to, and thought if I ever lost either of them, I would disappear.

"Oh good you're ready," Keegan greeted me with his trademark grin. He had mastered the art of appearances: pleasant smile, check, firm handshake, check, friendly demeanor, check. The villagers were captivated, and in a way, they had every right to be.

"Where are we going first?"

"Well, I thought first we could go through the hospital wing since your friend is staying here. It may give you more reassurance that he is under the best possible care."

I immediately knew what that really meant. He wanted to be sure that Cain saw me with him. But of course, I couldn't argue. So instead, I threw a layer of sugar over my words, anything to help get me to my ultimate goal: gaining his trust. "That is very considerate of you. I would like that very much." As we walked there, despite his calm expression, I could swear I felt his glee about Cain's suffering get deeper with every step.

It was almost frightening how much he was able to set up the hospital wing like a real hospital. From the monitors to the nurse's station, to the storage for medications, while it looked fairly outdated, it all seemed completely legitimate. Since it was an old military base, he must have had some supplies on hand to start with, but there were a lot of people in that village, and it was definitely a feat to keep everything so well-stocked and pristine. And since the building didn't start off as a hospital, he'd had to move everything there. I wondered if he was able to rebuild an entire hospital, what else he could pull off. He even bragged how he'd had the life-support systems wired to an emergency backup power generator, ensuring patient safety even if the electricity went down. With his resources and his charm, the possibilities were terrifyingly endless.

My stomach knotted tighter and tighter the closer we got to Cain's room. As it grew closer in the distance, I saw that someone had propped the door wide open.

Perfect. He wants to be sure Cain gets a good view.

As we crossed in front of the door, I fearfully glanced inside, enough to see the horror on Cain's face. My mouth went dry as Keegan did something to make it even worse. As we were in the middle of the doorway, he rested his hand on the small of my back. I could feel Cain's rage seeping through the air, and the guilt that flooded my body was almost enough to make me break away. I wanted to throw my arms around him and make sure he knew it was my idea, that I wasn't the one getting played. But I didn't. Instead, I let Keegan lead me down the stairs and out into his kingdom, leaving the man I loved to stew all alone.

The sun was bright, same as the day before, and

for just a split second when we first walked out, it burned my eyes. It was almost as if the weather itself was feeding into the illusion that Keegan had built…that the town was a perfect little oasis, where people didn't need to bother with protecting themselves because nothing bad could ever penetrate their defenses. It was plucked straight out of a kid's coloring book, a happy picture of children playing in the streets, and mothers looking on with kind, loving eyes.

If only they knew what was bubbling beneath the surface.

"Where would you like to go next?" he asked.

I decided I needed to wait for the right time to ask about the warehouse. That needed to be something to say toward the end of our tour when I had established as much of a friendly relationship with him as I could. Friendly was definitely a term I used loosely, but he didn't need to know that, and I prayed that he wouldn't if I could just behave myself. "The market looked like fun. Can we go there?"

"Ah! Excellent idea," Keegan said. "That is the busiest place in town. I will introduce you to some of the locals. I try to visit there once a day, to say hello to the people. Keeps me in tune with how they are feeling."

"And how are they feeling?" I winced at my words. Not exactly casual conversation.

"How are they feeling? Fantastic! Why wouldn't they be?" He paused to gesture at our surroundings. "Look around you, Riley. I have created something that's as close to the old America as anyone can remember. We even have generators around the village so some of the buildings other than the hospital have power. Some even have running water." He laughed. I almost snickered, thinking about the fact that the only buildings with electricity that I had noticed other than the hospital were the guards' quarters and food storage...oh, and the bar.

"We'd all like to think we can do without electricity, which we can, but we sure miss it when it's not around. And I couldn't very well have my house be the only one with it. Yes, it is the hospital too, but it just didn't seem right. It's stuff like that which make people loyal. That's the stuff that makes people stick around."

He *was* right about missing electricity and running water. Back at the compound, none of us had it. You get used to not having it after a while, but I'd be lying if I said I hadn't had some mornings where I would wake up from a dream of having my first hot shower in years, relishing in the feeling of the water running down my back, and it would disappear as quickly as it came. "Well, that was good of you to think of others." The words made me squeamish. I was sure there wasn't a moment in Keegan's life where he wasn't thinking of himself.

As we walked into the heart of the market I tried to get lost in it: the smells of hot grilled meats, the colors of all the vegetables sitting in neat little rows, the clink of metal upon metal as one piece was used to shape another. I tried to pretend I was there with Cain, relishing in the normalcy of it like we had been when we'd gone to the market in Rome. A shopping trip that most people would find wholly insignificant was something we would remember forever, something that gave us a taste of what I hoped we would have someday when the world had righted itself again. But instead, everything was turned on its side, and I was there with Keegan. It seemed as though everywhere we went, there was an outstretched hand of someone who wanted to thank "General Cole" for all he had done and continued to do to ensure their survival. Old women, young men, everyone seemed to step into our path to get a small taste of their leader's time. It made me sick.

"So tell me, Riley, how long have you been with this group of yours?"

"Didn't my mother tell you?"

"She didn't specify, just told me when you arrived at Father Dominic's compound." A panicked feeling swelled in my stomach. I was hoping he wasn't checking our stories to, make sure my mother had told the truth.

I hoped she really had been vague and prayed as I answered him. As much as I didn't want to give him any information, the question seemed harmless enough and I sure didn't want to contradict anything my mother had said. As furious as I was, I knew how much danger she was in and I had no desire to make it worse for her. The truth was my safest option. "We were there for four years."

"What did you do there?"

I didn't tell him I could fight. I would have much rather he figure that out when he found my knife aimed toward him; let him think I'm a weak little girl for as long as possible. I hoped that even though my mother seemed to have been fooled by him, she was at least smart enough to keep that part of our story to herself. "School mostly. It was really important to both me and Mom that I get an education, so that maybe if the country got better I could make a life for myself."

He smiled and squeezed my shoulder. It took all the willpower I had to not pull away. "Your mother is right. Maybe now you can find a place here. We could use someone smart like you to help us keep this place going. Running a village is no simple task, one reason why I'm so thankful for your mother's assistance."

I decided to ask the question I'd been dreading. "What exactly does she do here?"

"She hasn't told you?" I hoped I hadn't exposed myself, inadvertently letting him know that my mother and I weren't on good terms. "She's my right hand. If I'm not out here, she is, talking with the people, making sure everyone is happy, and finding problems before they become bigger problems."

I stopped short. "Problems? I thought you said everyone was happy."

He took my hands in his, playing the role of a protective father figure like a master. I wondered how many of his unsuspecting villagers found his hands around theirs and felt instantly soothed by the manufactured warmth in his voice. "It's impossible to make everyone happy, Riley. If your mother finds out someone is causing trouble, threatening what we've built, she tells me and we handle it."

After talking to Adam, I knew what handling it

meant. I shuddered to think about my mother hiding in corners, listening to unsuspecting victims, and using their words as their own poison, taking them back to Keegan like a damn carrier pigeon. "That's good I guess. Being proactive."

"That's right! Proactive." He slapped me on the back. "We'll make a leader out of you yet."

As we headed back toward the hospital/house, I notice that I could see what looked like the warehouses Adam had told us about peeking out in the distance. It was the perfect opportunity to ask Keegan what they were and merely sound curious rather than suspicious. "What are those buildings over there? Provisions or something?"

He glued on a smile. "Yes, provisions."

If I squinted hard enough, I could see a guard standing in front of one of them. "Guards need to look after fruits and veggies? Must be some good produce in there." I forced a giggle and noticed that though his grin never faded, the edges of it seemed to harden.

"We can't have people around here getting greedy. When people get greedy and want to take things for themselves, bad things happen, wouldn't you agree?"

I heard a veiled threat in his words. "Of course." I stared at him, making a veiled threat of my own. "When people get greedy, everything has a way of crashing down around them."

And if Cain and I had anything to say about it, everything would come crashing down around Keegan very soon.

CHAPTER SIX

Cain

Time moved slowly that day. I was stuck in the same minute over and over again; the one where I saw Keegan walking by my room with Riley. His hand was touching her, and if my body had been stronger I would have leaped out of bed and ripped it from his arm. It made my skin catch fire knowing that was exactly how he wanted me to feel: helpless. I found myself bargaining in my mind: *maybe I could leave this bed for just a moment, maybe I could just look out the window, just to see if she was alright.* But one glance at the tubes hanging from my flesh told me that neither of those things was an option.

I can't be sure if minutes or hours went by before I heard a knock. I expected to see Riley walk through the door and readied myself to hear an explanation for what I had seen earlier that day. But instead, I was faced with someone else. "Olivia. What are you doing here?" I didn't try very hard to hide my disappointment. I'm pretty sure I didn't even make eye contact, hoping she'd take the hint and go away.

Instead, she plopped herself down in the chair by my bed with a scowl on her face, evidently no more thrilled to be there than I was to have her. We weren't exactly each other's favorite company. "My shift. Don't worry, someone else should be here soon enough." She leaned back in her chair and rested her feet on one of the lower parts of my bed, crossing her legs one over the other like she was relaxing on the beach. "So, care to hurry up and get better so we can get out of here? I've been filled in and, needless to say, I've grown tired of this place."

"Believe me, I would love to. I'm trying my best." I hesitated before I spoke again, wondering if I would get a real answer from her instead of something that resembled gloating. "Is Riley back yet?"

"Nope. And hopefully not for a while."

"Why? What's going on?"

"She's trying to make sorta-friends with that Keegan guy to see if maybe he will give something up that we can use to get the hell out of here. That is if you'd buck up a little."

I sighed in relief. Riley had not been taken anywhere; she went of her own free will. And it was her idea in the first place. I still didn't like it, but it was better than the countless scenarios that had been playing in my mind since I had seen her. "How long has she been gone?"

"Since this morning."

The sick feeling returned as quickly as it had left.

"It's almost dark! Where the hell is she?"

I thought Olivia was going to give me more of an attitude but instead, her face softened, and she took her feet off my bed, looking me straight in the eyes as she did so. "You really do love her don't you?"

I nodded. "With every bit of who I am."

"She's perfectly capable of taking care of herself, but I know you know that." She sighed. "Tell you what. If she's not home in an hour, Reagan and I will go look for her, ok?"

I managed a smile. "Thank you." Though she could be a little snot, maybe there was a reason, other than misplaced loyalty, that Riley insisted on keeping Olivia around.

The next person to come in was Nick, slamming the door against the wall with the force of someone with a message that couldn't wait. "Cain! I would have been here sooner, but I couldn't get away from Keegan's guys in the town square. There's something you need to know. Riley's gone with Keegan to try to get information. I tried to talk her out of it but you know how she—"

Somehow right on cue, Riley threw the door open and ran toward me, throwing her arms around me and crunching my gunshot wound. I winced, but I didn't care. The pain was worth the embrace by a thousand miles. "Thank God! Are you all right?"

"I was just trying to get information, Cain, I'm so sorry. I never meant for you to see that."

Olivia piped in. "This one was worried sick about you. You shouldn't worry sick people you know."

Riley looked at her quizzically. "Was I mistaken,

or did I just hear you stand up for Cain? And *scold* me on his behalf on top of it?"

She shrugged and got up from her chair. "Truth is truth." Pointing to my torso, she said, "Why don't you sit down before you set him back a week. I'd like to be able to leave this place at *some* point."

Riley finally realized where she was leaning on me. "Oh, my gosh. I'm sorry."

I smiled as she sat down. "I'm just glad you're ok."

"I'll leave you two alone. Come on, Nick." Olivia nodded at me. "Goodnight, Cain."

"See you tomorrow, Cain. Goodnight." Nick hesitated for just a moment but followed.

After they left, Riley looked at me. "Are you two actually getting along?"

I smiled. "We discovered we have something in common."

"Like what?"

"We both love you."

She grabbed my hand. "I'm really sorry."

"Don't be." We sat there silently for a moment, savoring the fact that we were both there and both still alive. She leaned her head on the shoulder opposite my wound, and I inhaled the fresh scent of her hair. I learned over the years that those moments can be few and far between, and to relish in them when they arrived. But ultimately, life had a way of pushing its way through even the happiest seconds. I had to know, and as soon as I asked the question our peace was broken. "Did you find out anything?"

"Not sure. But he seems like he wants to involve me in his crew somehow after I've learned my way around. Probably for Mom's benefit, or just to keep an eye on me. I'll just conveniently never learn enough so I can avoid that one. But the biggest thing was there's definitely something in one of the warehouses at the other end of the village that he doesn't want us to see."

"Warehouses?"

"Yeah. You can't see them from here. He said they were food storage, but he has guards outside of one of them all day long and into the night. Ford mentioned them too. I think even he knows that there is something special hidden in there. Definitely more special than the produce he claims is in there. These people have plenty of food; they would have no reason to risk their lives to steal something they already have. I called Keegan on it but he didn't let anything slip. At least not yet."

Riley was right. Anything that Keegan had guarded that well had to be important, and possibly the key to making this little dictatorship he called salvation come tumbling down. "We have to get in that warehouse. I thought about something for a moment then realized we had no other choice. I didn't like bringing in someone I hadn't even met yet, but we needed someone who knew the place better than we did. "Talk to this Adam person tomorrow. With Jordyn. See if his people can help one of us get in there. There has to be some way to distract the guard long enough to at least get a peek."

"We're on it first thing tomorrow," Riley agreed.

"Fill in Nick and Dom too, you might need their help." Riley looked at me, and her bright eyes had turned sad. "What's wrong?"

"Nothing, I just want you to get better soon. I love those two but you and I are the team. We should be doing this together."

I squeezed her hand. "There's no one I trust more to get this done when I can't than you. You can do this."

"I know, but I don't want to have to." Her eyes welled up, but she quickly wiped them away. "Why does everything always have to be so hard?"

I pulled her toward me and kissed her. "Because we are who we are, and no one else can do this."

"Just promise me that someday, this can all be over."

"I promise." Even as the words slipped from my mouth, a part of me wondered if I was lying. Riley deserved the life of people who weren't like us, slow and steady and happy until the last day. But I feared that was something neither of us could achieve. After all we'd seen, all we'd done, I didn't know if there was a place for us there, in the quiet world that most people called home.

CHAPTER SEVEN

Riley

When Jordyn, Nick—he insisted on coming along—and I arrived at Adam's home the next day, we didn't exactly get a warm welcome. As he trimmed some empty green branches that weren't contributing to the tomato plant they were attached to, he said very flatly, "Get out."

"Adam, listen—"

He forcefully set his scissors down on his potting bench and turned toward us. "I saw you yesterday, wandering around here with that…man. You were talking like you were old friends." His forehead stiffened. "I mean how stupid do you think I am?"

"Look, dude, you don't know what happened. Let her talk," Nick said, stepping in front of me protectively.

"And another thing, who the hell is this guy? The point of a secret group *isn't* to have people shout about it from the rooftops. What are you doing, sending out telegrams about us? You might as well be making recruitment posters like General Cole." He pointed an angry finger at Nick, and his arm muscles tightened.

Jordyn pushed Nick back, willing him with her eyes to keep the posturing in check. "Nick's with us. We're all on the same side here." She stared into Adam's eyes. "Please, just listen to her."

Adam sighed. Even if Jordyn was abrasive, she was one of those people who even strangers knew they could trust. "You have one minute."

"Thank you," I said. I thought I might throw up and thanked myself for skipping breakfast. I hadn't talked about Cain's situation with a virtual stranger before. It felt a little bit like being ripped open. "That man is not who you think he is. General Cole doesn't exist. His name is Marcus Keegan.

Adam's face became white. "*The* Marcus Keegan? Former head of the Task Force Marcus Keegan? He was in charge of breaking up all those families. Mine included." He turned away for a moment and I wondered who had been stolen from him…who he had lost.

Maybe someday he will give me the privilege of knowing the name that belonged to the memory.

"The very same. He has changed his appearance substantially, but it's him. You know that first room on the corner of Keegan's building? The one that's in the hospital wing? Well, the man that I love is lying in bed up there. I don't know from one minute to the next if Keegan's going to decide to waltz right in there and take him away from me. He's already tried to kill him once before."

"I'm listening."

"We know Keegan is an evil man. I don't believe for a second that he's made some sort of miraculous turnaround from the person he used to be. I'm trying to use the fact that my mother is with him to gain his trust, or at least something resembling trust in the hopes that he will accidentally give me some clue what is really going on here and how we can get out of here safely. Keegan's not going to let us go without a fight; that much we know for sure."

"Wait a minute, you're Claire Crane's daughter?"

I worried I had stepped over the line, but his face softened. "She's the only one who has ever shown any of us mercy, or at least convinced Cole to. Some of us wouldn't still be here without her, that much I'm sure of." I felt myself grow still. His account of my mother's position was nowhere close to Keegan's version. Maybe the mother I knew was still inside her somewhere. I searched my memory of our last conversation for anything that may have told me I was wrong, something that I had missed. I found nothing but disappointment and shame, but this new information from Adam made me think that perhaps it was time to have a little faith. Adam extended his hand. "So, tell me what you need from me."

"We need to get into that warehouse. I'm sure you know which one I mean."

Adam hesitated. "It'll be very dangerous. Are you sure it's necessary? We might not all make it without getting thrown in jail…or worse."

Nick piped in. "Absolutely. We need to know what we're up against before we do this thing."

Shattered Night

"Do what?"

"Bring the sonofabitch down."

Adam told us that the easiest way to get into the warehouse would be during the time when one particular guard was on duty at the back of the building. He had studied the guards long enough to know that one of them had a habit of taking an unauthorized smoke break during the first part of his shift. "We have to be stone-cold silent. Our best bet is the window at the back of the building. It's the lowest of all of them. We won't risk going inside, just need to be able to see what's in there. A quick look, then we're out."

"Makes sense. Nick, you, me, and Dom can go. Two of you can keep watch while the other lifts me up so I can see."

Jordyn looked insulted. "What about me?"

I put my hands on her shoulders. "Someone needs to stay behind in case God forbid something goes wrong. If it does, he'll go straight to Cain and it could all be over. There's no one I trust more to protect him than you. If it goes bad, get Olivia and Reagan and take Cain as far away from this place as you can."

She bit her lip but almost immediately straightened herself back into business mode. "I understand. And you know I will."

I hugged her tight. "Thank you."

"So when is this going to happen?" She asked.

I looked at Adam. "I think we need to let some time pass from my outing with Keegan so no one gets suspicious, just to be safe."

"Three days?"

"Ok. You guys good with that?" I looked at Jordyn and Nick. They both gave their approval. "All right." I gestured toward Adam. "We will follow you from a distance, so he doesn't see you with us."

"Ok. I will see you soon. Until then, don't come by again."

The three of us shook his hand and headed out into the afternoon.

When we got back to our room, Jordyn looked at me and smiled. "What?" I asked.

"I hope you know that Cain would be proud of how you handled that today. So am I. I think you're out of your sloppy funk."

I looked at her, in the way a little sister looks at a big sister who had finally given her a compliment. I always knew Jordyn was proud of me, but she'd never been the sentimental type. I hung on to her praise tightly knowing how fleeting it may be. "Thank you. That means a lot. Especially coming from you."

Jordyn smirked. "Don't get all soft on me now, we have a lot of work to do, and soon." Suddenly her face grew serious. "Do you think…"

"What?"

"Do you think we could trust your mother to distract him? Even if she doesn't approve of what we're doing she'd want to protect us." She finished her sentence as more of a question than a statement.

I sat down on my bed and ran my hands over the soft bedspread. "We can't risk it. I'd like to think she still would, but I just don't know anymore. I mean Jordyn she actually compared Cain to him.

Shattered Night

Can you imagine? How would she think that would make me feel? Make *him* feel?"

"You're right, that really doesn't sound like her." She sat down next to me. "I guess we will have to do this on our own."

I started to stare out the window. "Do you ever get tired of fighting?"

She wrapped her arms around me and squeezed me tight. "Honestly, I hate to say it, but even after meeting Micah, it's all come back to me as if it never left. That instinct. Don't get me wrong, if circumstances had been different, I could have stayed at that compound with Micah and McKenzie and died a happy old woman. But the fighter was never dead, she just laid dormant, waiting for when she was needed again."

My fighter hadn't been dormant for a very long time.

***

Those three days passed by slowly, between visits with Cain, and painfully shared meals with Keegan and his higher-ups. Every once in a while, I would take a chance and glance at my mother, hoping to get some clue, some hint of the woman who I had seen before we had left for Italy.

But I didn't.

Instead, I saw a woman smiling and leaning her head against Keegan's shoulder as he reveled in telling her stories about his supposed days as a general. I knew she realized they weren't true, but she seemed to enjoy them all the same. She appeared like a child listening to her father read her fairy tales, even though she was old enough to know they didn't exist, just wanting to hear about the elves and castles one more time. I tried to take comfort in what Adam had told me, but from the display I saw in front of me, just because she bent the rules to help people out didn't mean that Keegan didn't have her completely fooled. You can think a rule is unfair but still care for the person who made it and she looked like she cared for him deeply.

Dom, Nick, and I met Adam in the middle of town, hoping that the thickness of the afternoon crowds would hide us as we made our way to the warehouse. We slipped through the rows of homes and buildings, sticking in the shadows just as Cain would have, following behind Adam so as not to be seen together. I could feel Cain willing us on from his hospital bed, wishing he could be by our sides as much as we yearned to have him there. It reminded me of how I felt when I would secretly practice throwing my knife at a tree before he had returned when I would hear his voice in the whisper of my footsteps.

As we neared the warehouse, the crowd dissipated into a sprinkling of people, leaving us without our cover. We hoped it had lasted long enough to protect us and clustered closer together, figuring that we needed all of us near each other, so we could protect each other's blind corners. We carefully kept our eyes out for anyone who worked for Keegan, scanning the area around us as carefully as we could. "Everyone pick it up. We don't have much time before our new favorite guard shows up," Adam said low enough so that only our group could hear.

"Right, but if we get there early they're going to wonder why we are hanging around," Nick countered.

"You're both right," I hissed at each of them. "Let's just keep moving."

The warehouse we were after began growing in the distance, and we were upon it quicker than we anticipated. Luckily, there was an embankment by the creek that ran the length of the town right in front of the warehouse, so we were able to hide below the hill. The guard at the front had his nose deep down in the pages of something that looked like a magazine from far away; something that I doubted Keegan would approve of, but it allowed us to sneak down to our hiding spot. Dom and I sat just at the edge, able to keep an eye on things but stay unseen. "Are you ready to see whatever we are going to find here?" he asked.

I paused for a moment. "Honestly...no. But I know it has to be done. Whatever he's got behind those doors is going to decide what happens to us as well as the rest of these people. Hell, it could be even worse than that. We can't not know."

He nodded. His strong and sure expression had become cautious and worrisome. "I feel the same way. A part of me wants to hold on to this moment, the time before we know what we were up against. But I realize it can't wait."

Seeing a bit of vulnerability in Dom was somehow comforting. If someone who had carried us all for so long could be frightened, I didn't feel as guilty about not really wanting to climb back up the hill and face what we were about to see. I reached over and locked his fingers in mine. Without Cain there, Dom's support helped me keep my sanity more than anything else. "We're going to be ok, no matter what is up there." Though I said it, my heart wasn't sure if I meant it.

He agreed then looked back at Nick and Adam. "Here we go."

Sure enough, the guard we were waiting for was on duty for only about ten minutes before he left his post for a cigarette. It was then that we made our approach. I shivered at every crunch of the dry, brown grass under our feet, praying that one or two blades of it didn't give us away and land us in jail. I didn't want to know what could happen in there. Having one of us there would be a perfect playtime for Keegan, a golden opportunity to torture Cain just a little bit more. He'd already almost killed Nick and Dom before; there's no telling what he would do ten years later. My fear for them started to make me change my mind and wish that we hadn't come at all. I ached to look around and discover we were just back in our rooms, thinking and hoping something would change. But we were never the ones who had the luxury of sitting by. That task was for other people, innocents who didn't know how to fight. We were always the ones who had to tilt the world right again, no matter what the cost.

Adam faced the left of us and Nick faced the right, making sure if a guard came our direction we would have time to run; though honestly there would have been nowhere for us to go.

Shattered Night

I stared up at the small, metal framed window that held our fate. As Dom lifted me up, I carefully maneuvered my feet onto his massive shoulders, using the side of the building to support myself. I then grabbed the edge of the window. I pulled as Dom pushed, and somehow, I was able to lift myself to where I could see what lay beyond the glass.

Much louder than I meant to, I gasped. The disaster in front of me was as terrible as I could have imagined. Lying there, so unsuspectingly, so innocently, was something that had the potential to bring about total annihilation in an already fragile land.

Helicopters.

The helicopters themselves weren't the issue. There had to be other people in America, although very few, that had air transportation. It was the fact that *Keegan* had air transportation. That gave him a method to travel long distances, and if he so desired, mobilize his quest for power, where he could spread his poison across the country.

After seeing the near-perfect condition of the hospital, I should have known that assuming he only had access to working ground vehicles was naïve. We were on an old military base, and in a village as big as his there had to be at least a couple who knew how to fly aircraft, and he had enough resources to recruit other pilots. Also, with as many supply runs as he sent his men on, they probably have enough siphoned gas saved up to take him as far as he wanted to go.

A mobile Keegan would be more dangerous than

anything we'd ever seen.

Keegan had a dozen, lined up in two rows, their main rotors removed and carefully stowed underneath. Most were white with a blue stripe, but one was painted in all red. The rest weren't military helicopters, at least not ones I was familiar with. They looked more like the kind used by newscasts and sightseers, except they'd all been modified with machine guns mounted on either side.

Quickly, without a second thought, I grasped the side of the window and slid it open. It hit the other side with a thud. I heard Dom's desperate voice below me as I pulled myself up and through the window. "What are you doing? Riley, there's no time!"

"I have to get a closer look. Don't wait for me."

I landed on some storage containers just below the window. My shoulder took most of the pressure from the fall, and I winced as I landed, imagining the bones sliding against each other. I took one last second to carefully get to my knees and shut the window on my friends behind me. Like many other times in my life, I could hear Cain in my head— *What you're doing right now is really fucking stupid. If they don't kill you, I will. Climb back out the window before it's too late.*

Sorry, Cain.

As quietly as I could, I climbed down the shelf that held the storage containers and made my way to the floor of the warehouse. I ducked behind it and listened for a minute or so, hoping there weren't guards on the inside as well as the outside. I was alone, at least for the moment.

Shattered Night

I decided to look in the red helicopter, taking a guess that the one different one would be Keegan's. Inside, there were several crates labeled "food," "medicine," and "water," along with several guns. Multiplying the number of guns by the number of helicopters, I realized there was enough firepower inside to take out a village the size of the one we were in, maybe even bigger.

There was something else there too, something that told me more than even the guns did. A list sat on the pilot's chair, attached to a clipboard. On each sheet of paper were names, occupations, and flight dates. The first one listed the doctor's name, and as I looked further, I realized all the people listed who weren't guards had two things in common: they were valuable, and they were all living very comfortable lives, more than most of the other citizens in the village, thanks to Keegan.

As I flipped through the pages, Keegan's plan took shape.

The population was getting out of hand in the village, which gave Keegan the perfect reason to search the country for other places to settle his people, under the guise of a caring ruler. He could pick places with shaky leadership, with people who were more likely to welcome a new person willing to take charge. Keegan and his men would arrive at one of those particular clusters of people scattered across America, bearing gifts and hopes of being able to bring in a few of their own citizens…at first. Especially when the people he was bringing were people they needed: doctors, firefighters, welders…why would they say no? Keegan was practically gift wrapping them. They would shower people with precious cans of vegetables, antibiotic ointment, and drinking water that they didn't have to boil to make sure it was safe…all very attractive to people who had to struggle to feed themselves for years. He could plant people who he already knew were loyal to him in amongst the new villages, making his transition to power even easier. Those people would sing his praises to the other villagers, and when he came back to take power, an invasion from a man who had a smoothly-running village would look like a favor. And if that didn't work, or didn't work fast enough, he could move on to plan B, the guns, with plenty of ammo to destroy anyone who didn't fall in line, and without anyone from his own village who would protest.

He wasn't just planning to stick to this one village, he wanted it all. And unless we could stop him, he had all the firepower and, as evident by looking around the village, all the charisma he needed to get it. And there was no telling what the country would become after that.

President Marcus Keegan.

As far as we knew, everyone in the normal system of government who would have been in line for the presidency had been killed, though it wasn't like there was a system of government anymore anyway. Keegan really didn't need to be anywhere in line for the spot, he just needed to be the most powerful guy around. And from the looks of it, he was.

I made my way through each one of the helicopters and found the same setup as the first:

gifts for the cooperative, bullets for the troublemakers. I looked around the supply area of the warehouse, trying to find something to cut the wires in the helicopters with. I had no idea which wire did what, but I figured they all had to be important, and if I could get his firepower all out of commission it would at least buy us some more time. At that moment, I didn't care if he figured out it was me, just that I stopped him. But as I was about to search through another drawer, I heard a door at the front of the warehouse open. A voice said, "Yeah, General Cole wants us to sweep the warehouse, but he didn't say why. Kind of random but I guess you can be as random as you want when you're the boss."

He knows we're here. Somehow he knows we're here.

"Not random at all. He's been doing that recently. Said he's trying to make sure he can trust some of the new villagers," the second voice said.

Of course, I thought. Keegan was smart. I'd slipped up asking about the warehouse when he and I had our tour—I had tipped my hand, and I was about to pay for it.

I held my breath as I listened to their footsteps, careful to move as they did, but in the opposite direction. I was doing ok until the men split up, one going one direction, and one going the other. As I found myself curled up, ducking behind a crate near the first plane by the door, I knew I was in trouble. A set of footsteps came toward me, but I couldn't go anywhere without the second man seeing me in an instant. Just as I thought I would be caught for sure, I was jolted by the sound of something being slammed against the metal wall of the warehouse. Both men who were looking around glanced at each other instead and ran out the door, their guns drawn. At a safe distance, I followed them. As their backs were turned, I took a second to look and see what had driven them out of the warehouse.

Nick was standing there in handcuffs, with Adam lying on the ground, blood dripping from his nose. "What are you arresting me for? He started it!" Nick said as he writhed against his restraints, red hair sticking against his forehead with sweat. I saw him see me and give me a subtle wink, and as I mouthed a thank you, tears formed at the edge of my eyes.

"I don't care who started it. You're spending the night in a cell. We don't tolerate that shit around here."

Yeah right.

I slipped away from the warehouse, meeting Dom behind the first one in the line, the one furthest away from my would-be captors. Apparently, none of them had listened when I told them not to wait for me.

Thank God.

"What were you thinking? You could have gotten caught and this would have all been over!"

I grabbed his hand and pulled him behind the structure that served as the town bar, located just before the warehouses. "Dom, it's bad. Really bad. And Nick…" I couldn't even finish my sentence, because I knew if I did, the tears wouldn't stop. I took a couple of deep breaths and willed myself to keep calm.

He took a deep breath as though he was going to continue yelling at me but restrained himself. "What did you see?"

I described the helicopters, the guns, and provisions, and of course, the passenger lists, everything Keegan could use to mount a cross-country takeover, also telling him about the random searches, and my suspicion that I caused them by asking about the warehouse on my outing with Keegan. "So it is as bad as we suspected. Actually, worse."

"Yes." I paused for a second. "Dom, I'll need to somehow sneak back in and cut some of the wiring to dismantle them."

He shook his head. "No, way too risky. If you get caught again, we're all done for, and Cain is still not ready to leave the hospital. Even when he is, Keegan's going to have his eye on us now more than ever. We'll never get the chance."

I had to admit he was right. "Ok, well what do we do then? This *can't* happen."

Dom stared at me hard. "Riley, we are in way over our heads. There's just not enough of us. If we take this on, there's a good chance not all of us are going to make it out alive. I can't bear the thought of losing any one of you." He paused and grabbed my face in his hands. "We've all fought for other people for a long time now. Maybe this one is somebody else's fight."

I gently pulled his hands away. "If not us, Dom, who? I'm willing to bet he's the only one in the entire country with this kind of power. There *is* no one else."

He stared at me, considering for a moment. "There still aren't enough of us. We need help."

"I know." That was one thing that he was right about. And I had no idea how we were going to get it.

That night, I filled in Cain and Jordyn about everything that happened. Surprisingly enough, the guards were true to their word and Nick knocked on our door the following morning a free man. His eye was swollen shut, and there was some bruising on his torso where it looked like he'd been kicked, but he seemed ok. When I saw him, I apologized over and over again and hugged him tight. "They told me to behave myself," he said, snickering. "If only they knew."

We told Nick everything I saw, and about my conversation with Dom he night before. "We know we need help, we just don't know what to do to get it."

Nick sighed, as if the answer was right in front of our faces. "Leave that to me."

"How?"

"If I can get out of here, I can reach out to the guide network. When they hear what's going on, I'm sure a ton of them will be ready to go. I'm sure they'll all be itching for a little payback too."

Olivia had been listening the whole time, but only then spoke up. "Um, hate to break it to you, but after yesterday, you're already on their keep-an-eye-on-that-guy list. How are you going to get out of here?"

Nick smirked. "I have no idea but I'll tell you

I'm damn well going to figure it out one way or another."

"I don't know, Nick. Keegan's not going to want any of us to leave, that much is clear. There's no telling what he will do if you go."

"We will just have to wait until Cain is better. Then after that, it's a risk we're going to have to take. Or this dude is going to be going all fighter-pilot on us before we know it. Dom, tell her."

Dom hesitated before he spoke. "If you all are dead set on doing this, we do have a better chance with more people. Nick, damn it be careful, whatever you do. I want you in one piece when this is over."

Nick smiled and ran his fingers through his wavy red hair. "Always."

Suddenly, Olivia piped in again. "By the way, Reagan is starting to wonder why everyone is avoiding him and Ford. Shouldn't we tell them what's going on?"

It was a risk, but she was right. We had kept them in the dark for as long as we could, and time was running out. Ford may be able to help, and I really hated keeping them both out of everything we were doing. "You're right, Liv, but let me talk to Ford first. I have to make sure he remembers who he can trust and who he can't. He's a little too happy here and that concerns me a lot."

Jordyn shook her head. "I don't like it, Riley, he's changed. He may be lost to us."

"That may be true, but he would never hurt us. He won't betray us for anybody, even Keegan. He may not help us, but he won't hurt us. Ever."

"Ok. I hope you're right."

I hoped I was too. Because if not, we would be finished before we got started.

CHAPTER EIGHT

Riley

For the next month, there was nothing we could do but wait. Cain was gradually getting better, and we knew we couldn't make any sort of move until he was well. I spent my time watching my mother with Keegan, the way they held hands, the way she gazed at him when I knew for a fact he couldn't see her. I wondered if she had ever looked at Bo that way or my father for that matter. I searched my memory for just one single image, just one to let me know that was just the way she looked at men, that it was all part of her natural charm.

I came up with nothing and started to question whether I knew her at all.

I had tried several times to talk to Ford, but he was constantly working (or constantly telling me he was working. After a while, I couldn't be sure which). This meant that Reagan remained in the dark and kept walking in on us talking as a group without him. Unfortunately, this pushed him even closer to Ford, and I grew concerned that he would ask to join him as a guard. By some miracle though, my mother hired him first to be her assistant. He would be with her when she interacted with the villagers, so they could report back to Keegan. And if any of the villagers got angry with her for any reason, he would be by her side. I wasn't very happy about it, but it was better than him joining Ford in the deepest part of Keegan's organization.

The day Cain left the hospital wing was the best day of my life. We had to keep our distance because he insisted we downplay our relationship to try to undo the damage he had done in that first meeting with Keegan. I tried to convince him it would be fine, but he wouldn't hear of it. So, when he left his bed to rejoin the world, Dom pushed him in a wheelchair—although he didn't need one, the doctor insisted—toward their room, and I was left to sleep in my bed alone.

When I said goodnight that night, I kissed him so longingly I'm pretty sure everyone turned away; either out of respect or disgust…probably a bit of both. With our friends in the background, he smiled a smile that signaled to me the end of one thing, and the beginning of something else. "I love you. I'll see you tomorrow. Tomorrow everything changes."

I kissed him one more time. "I hope not."

Cain smiled and kissed my forehead. "Well, not *everything*."

I stared at him for as long as I could when I closed the door, lingering as the crack got smaller and smaller. As I clicked it shut, I swallowed hard, not wanting to give up the image of the man I love

Shattered Night

alive and well, surrounded by people I knew would die to protect him. We'd been through so many life and death situations, I couldn't help but wonder if eventually, we would stop coming out the other side.

The next day, I had Nick and Jordyn tail Keegan for the morning so that Cain and I could have a chance to talk about what the next step would be. If Keegan headed back to our hall, one of them would warn me before we were seen. Cain was still in bed when I got to their room. When he opened his eyes, he pulled me down next to him. "We are supposed to be focusing on getting out of here," I giggled.

"Come on, you know it's been far too long. And how many opportunities are we going to get for this sort of thing when both of us have a cluster of roommates?"

Grinning, I said, "Good point."

He pulled the covers over us and we got reacquainted in a way that we hadn't been able to since Italy. As I lay there in his arms, I was finally able to forget where we were, the storm we were about to walk into, and everything we had to lose.

It always seems like life has a way of placing the most horrifying things right beside the most beautiful. Because as we lay there in a moment of peace that was few and far between, a knock at the door jolted us out of it as quickly as it had arrived. I said goodbye to the quiet as I hid under the covers, and Cain yelled, "Come in."

It was Dom. "You better come quickly. Something big is happening in the middle of town."

"What?" Cain asked.

"Hanging. There's a bunch of people down there." Dom said he had heard whispers around town about hangings, but a part of him had hoped it had just been drunk-talk or the ramblings of people who were accustomed to exaggeration. I didn't have the heart to tell him that Adam had confirmed the rumors, and I had known something like this was coming for quite a while. At that moment, Dom found out how very wrong he was.

"You're serious? And there's several of them?" Cain asked.

"Unfortunately, yes."

"Be right out."

"Oh, and Cain, tell Riley to get dressed and come too."

I felt my face turn red under the covers. I suppose there wasn't really much point in hiding there when my clothes were scattered all over the floor, but I figured it was always polite to try.

Cain and I raced downstairs, mere steps behind Dom. He had us follow him to where Nick, Reagan, Olivia, and Jordyn were standing in amongst the crowd. I glanced up to see what everyone was staring at. Nestled in the dust swirling at our feet, gallows rose up like a lighthouse from the flattened landscape. It looked as though it could be wheeled in and out, able to be hidden away when there wasn't anyone that they deemed deserving of death. I supposed a hanging platform would take away from the peaceful, harmonious picture that Keegan had created. Apparently, he didn't mind a horror show as long as it was strategically placed. There were not one, but several people standing on the

Shattered Night

platform with thick ropes around their necks, and black hoods over their faces. Some of them were thrashing about, making one more attempt to free themselves from a death that, given all the bystanders were surrounded by Keegan's men, seemed inevitable. I heard a few cry out, words they may have wanted to say muffled by what sounded like gags in their mouths. There were also two extra ropes, hanging there unoccupied. It seemed strange until I realized why. Keegan was trying to remind everyone in that crowd that if they didn't live by the rules, *his* rules, perhaps they would be next. *The next rope could be yours*, I imagined him thinking to himself as he watched the crowd around him. I felt myself inch closer to Cain, and to push the fear out of my gut, I grabbed his hand.

Despite our desire to keep up appearances, he didn't let go.

"What did these people do?" I asked a woman in a long dress standing beside us, clutching her son to her.

"We don't know yet. The general doesn't tell us until it's about to happen."

I glanced at Cain. "Do we know when it's going to happen exactly?" he asked her.

She looked toward her right and saw Keegan emerging from the crowd, flanked by four guards, one of them Ford. "Looks like right about now."

I took a risk and hoped it wouldn't cost me dearly: I voiced dissent. "And no one says anything? They just let this happen?"

The woman stared at me, unblinkingly. "Look around you. We have food, shelter, a place to stay.

Before we got here those are things a lot of us hadn't had in a very long time." She paused. "As long as it's not me, or part of my family, I'm not saying a word."

I considered arguing with the woman, but instead, I watched. As Keegan and his guards moved through the square, people automatically moved out of his way, giving them plenty of space. I saw him shake the hands of people as he passed, his face pleasant but somber, the perfect expression for such an event, as if to say, *No one wants this to happen but it has to be done.*

He pointed to the platform. "My fellow citizens—these people attacked a group of our guards on the way home from a supply run. These guards are part of our village family. And what do you do when someone hurts your family? You cut them off and make sure they can never harm them again." From the looks of everyone around the platform, they were all buying it, but there was no doubt in my mind there was more to the story of what was about to happen to these people. I watched as a group of people who were centuries ahead in time from Medieval Europe, centuries away from the Wild West, reverted to their sadistic ancestry for an afternoon of blood.

He stepped onto the platform toward the front middle, letting his guards surround him from the ground on all sides. "Friends—citizens, today is a hard day for all of us. Despite these people causing us harm, we are still human beings. No one wants to see a life end, but as we all know after the struggles and hardships we have faced while building our

Shattered Night

new home, if we let our enemies gain control, we will lose everything. This will no longer be a place where we can spend our days in peace. We will give up the reassurance that we fought so hard to attain—the reassurance that means our children are safe and out of harm's way. They deserve to grow up with the innocence that we seemed to have lost so long ago." He took a deep breath, probably to seem like the task ahead was exhausting to him. "These people have stolen something from us—our security. Look around you. Do you think we need someone else to decide how we live our lives? To take away the life we earned for ourselves?"

"No!" I heard shouts from the crowd.

"Do you think anyone could take care of us better than we are taking care of ourselves?"

"No!"

"That's right. Our village is our home. We must protect it and our way of life here. And unfortunately, that means we must snuff out those who would seek to destroy us, no matter how much it pains us to do so."

As he spoke, my stomach twisted tighter and tighter around itself. It took me a moment to realize why, and when I did, I had to step away from everyone for a moment to throw up. Jordyn and Cain automatically stood in front of me to block people's view as we all heard the vomit land softly in the dirt at my feet. When I turned around, they were staring at me. "Are you ok?" Cain asked as he rubbed my back.

"This speech. It's my mother. My mother wrote that."

The words coming out of Keegan's mouth had a tone that was all too familiar to me, the tone that had helped destroy the country in the first place. And now she was using it to help Keegan? The thought made me tremble. She could not have figured out a way to wound me more deeply than that. But I had to momentarily stuff the feeling down because from over Cain's shoulder I could see one of the guards grasping the lever that would send all those people to their deaths.

The snap of the platform falling away seemed to echo in the quiet. The people dangling from the ends of the ropes instinctively kicked their feet in the air, their bodies trying to win the fight that their minds could not. The sickness that filled each of us as we watched their bodies slowly grow still over an agonizing minute was like nothing I had ever experienced, their deaths more real than any of the others I had seen at the edge of my blade.

The seven of us stood silently as the crowd thinned out, their thirst for violence quenched for the day. Sure, they didn't hang those people, but at that moment, I couldn't help but hate them. I knew why we were there, why we couldn't risk stopping him, but the rest of them…to stand by and just watch? It made me wonder why we were planning on risking our lives to help set them free, free from bonds that they seemed very comfortable in, or as the woman had said, as long as it wasn't her or her family. But then I had to remember that though we were there for a reason, though we had a plan that we had to follow through with at all costs, I *had* been standing right beside them. I began to imagine what those people hanging on the ends of those ropes would have to say about the worthiness of our plan versus the value of their lives.

"He wanted them to suffer," I heard Dominic whisper from behind me.

"What do you mean?"

He pointed to the platform. "Historically, those are supposed to be designed to snap a person's neck instantly. They weren't supposed to slowly choke to death." He took a deep breath. "He did that on purpose." I gently grabbed his arm in an attempt at comfort, but after what we had just witnessed, I knew there was nothing I could do. The pain that I knew was weighing deep in Dom's heart was resting heavily in mine too.

After the crowd and Keegan were both gone, the guards started gathering the bodies and loading them into the back of a truck that had pulled up. As Ford put the last body in, I marched up to him and pushed him hard in his chest. "How could you be a part of this? How could you? It's disgusting. You're putting on the same spectacle for people that they did in the dark ages. What's wrong with you? You aren't the person I've known for years. You're something else."

He attempted to hold me still, so I couldn't strike him again, but I wriggled free. "It's part of my job, Riley. There was nothing I could do."

I was about to argue with him when my heart stopped cold; because out of the corner of my eye, I saw something glistening from the bed of the truck. I marched passed Ford to see what it was, and the closer I got, the faster my heart started beating.

There was a ring on the hand of the last victim. This person had been standing on the far end of the platform. With shaking hands, I slid the ring off the lifeless finger. I could barely control my knees, willing them to not buckle.

I had to be sure.

I forced myself to pry the black hood off him. As I lifted it free, I found what I was praying I wouldn't: Jordyn's husband Micah's vacant eyes staring back at me, the life gone but the kindness in their gaze still lingering behind. The man that had given Jordyn a chance to love, to feel normal, the man who had sung her to sleep at night, the person she had pledged to love now and forever was dead.

And we had watched him die.

I braced myself against the truck as everyone came over to see why I had almost collapsed, Jordyn leading the way. Quickly—desperately—I took his ring off so she wouldn't see it, stood back up and tried to block her view. "Jordyn, please, you don't want to see this. Let's go back to the room and talk."

She stared at me. "What the hell are you talking about? Why would you…" She paused. "You knew…we knew them?" Within a second, I saw her eyes change. I saw the exact moment she realized that her world had crumbled, and I was trying to give her a few spare minutes of not realizing it. Shoving me away, she gave herself full view of her husband lying in a pile of corpses, thrown without a care in the back of a truck as if he never mattered to anyone. The people who had helped dispose of him…they would never know the way he held his daughter's hand, or how he smiled proudly at his bride on their wedding day. To them, he was nothing more than a load they had to carry away from town, to erase the mess before the brutality of what we had just witnessed sank in. "No...no, no, no, no, no...it can't be. He was supposed to be back at the safe house where we left them, back by the water where McKenzie could see the beach." She grabbed his face in her hands and shook him hard. "Wake up. Please wake up!" Cain came up behind her, eyes wide and full of suffering as he realized what had happened, and grabbed her around the waist, slowly pulling her away from the truck.

"Let me go! It's not him. Let me go! No! Let me go!" She wailed, thrashing around in Cain's arms so hard he could barely hang on to her. Nick and Dom stood on either side and attempted to help hold onto her as best they could while they lead her away, letting Reagan follow next to them and keep a lookout. They took her in the opposite direction of the house where we were staying, probably figuring that if she saw Keegan there's no telling what she might do, let alone what he would do in return. Had he killed Jordyn's husband just to torture us? Or was this the final blow before the next set of ropes would find their way around our necks?

When they were out of sight, I let myself fall right where Jordyn had been, clutching Micah's ring tightly in my hand. Instead of my mother comforting me while I was afraid, it was now Olivia who sat right next to me in the dirt and threw her arms around me, letting me cry. I laid my head on her shoulder and let her play with my hair, trying to get lost in the gesture while my insides felt as if an avalanche had started, never to be stopped.

Ford hovered over us, and though he was one of the last people I wanted to see, having another familiar presence there was somewhat comforting. With Verita still back on the island, and Micah now gone, there weren't many of us left. I looked up at him, my face red and swollen. "What do you think of your precious general now?"

He didn't answer, but suddenly his face lost all color. I saw him climb in with the bodies and start rummaging around. At first, I didn't understand what he was doing until I realized he was trying to pry off the hoods on all the rest of the bodies. My heart sped up again as I watched him destroy us deeper one hood at a time. Staring back at us was Jordyn's mother Natalie, Reagan's parents, and last, Ford's own parents. His big, thick hands started trembling when he saw the faces of his mother and father. "Oh my God. My mom…dad…they're gone." He clenched his fists and bowed his head. Maybe he hoped when he raised it again the sight before him would be different. "It's our whole group. He found them all."

He turned away, his strong exterior marred by the tears of a man who knew he had lost–the mother and father who had given him life were now nothing more than a shadow, only existing in the memories that would have to feed him for the rest of his life. Olivia and I pulled him down and made him sit with us on the ground. I could feel his body shaking with the kind of force usually brought on by a deep chill. "The kids aren't there. Xander and

McKenzie aren't there. Maybe they're still—"

"Riley, I'm so sorry. This is all my fault."

I threw my arms around him. "No, Ford, it's not. Don't say that. It's that bastard in charge. We need to tell you that—"

"No, Riley." He turned to face me, normally bright eyes reddened. "I know who he is. Claire told me."

"What?"

"She gave me a letter, to get to you through the guide network, to warn you not to come here. You were supposed to find somewhere else or stay somewhere close until she and I could meet up with you safely." He took a deep breath. "Riley, I threw the letter in the garbage. That's how you ended up here. That's why all those people are dead."

I sat there, stunned and angry all at once. "Why? God, why would you do that?"

"Because look at this place! It looked safe, and normal, and happy. All I had to go on to tell me that this wasn't real was some story from Cain's past, just his word that the General...Keegan...wasn't what he appeared. I wasn't going to let you have an opportunity for a normal life snatched away from you just based on the word of some asshole that I didn't trust from the beginning. I wanted to give you a chance to see for yourself. I was trying to protect you, from him, from everything else. I was trying to give you a shot at something different."

Suddenly, everything made sense. My mother hadn't gone crazy. I didn't know why she had pretended to believe Keegan's lies, but in truth, she was still one of us. But that relief was short lived as

I looked in the face of the man who had once been one of my best friends, the man who had betrayed us all and cost Jordyn her husband.

I didn't even have the strength to yell. But sometimes, being quiet conveys more than yelling ever could. Yelling means there's a chance for forgiveness; silence means that hope is long gone. I turned to Olivia, and said calmly, evenly, "Will you please take me back to the room?" She nodded and helped me to my feet.

"Riley, please talk to me. Say something. Scream at me. Anything."

Olivia turned toward him and slapped him across the face. "Shut up, and stay away from her. You've done enough."

"My parents are dead too! We've all lost! All of us!" He screamed after us, desperately, but seemed to know not to follow, standing there under the deceptively beautiful evening sky.

I let her practically carry me back to our room, not taking one second to look back at the man who had just cost six people their lives. Olivia and I agreed not to tell anyone about the letter. It wouldn't help Jordyn to find out that one of her friends unintentionally set events in motion that ended with Micah's death. Now I had a taste of what my mother felt when we found out what Bo had done so many years ago. Yes, he betrayed our trust to protect her, but the trust was broken nonetheless, and on the backs of people we cared for deeply.

When Olivia and I arrived, everyone was congregated in our room looking after Jordyn. We walked in to see her pushing everything off the shelves and onto the floor. Glass shattered everywhere into little useless shards. Our dressers fell hard, and clothes spewed out across the wooden surface. Solid reds, blues, and whites, stripes, and dots lie lifelessly around us. The boys looked on, as if they had considered trying to stop her, then thought the better of it. When she had run out of things to destroy, she collapsed into a heap on the floor. I rushed over to her and held her to me. "I'm so sorry, Jordyn."

She looked up at me with a tear-stained face and redness in her cheeks. The words that came next were not those I had expected, but something far worse. "You shouldn't be sorry. *He's* the one that should be sorry." I followed her line of sight to see who she was directing her accusation.

She was staring straight at Cain.

CHAPTER NINE

Keegan

I was staring at our supply inventory logbook when Ford entered the room, making the door slam against the wall in his wake. I expected as much. He had every right to be upset. I had just had his parents and those of his best friend murdered.

But he didn't need to know that.

"Ford...I'm so sorry. I only just found out." I felt his fingers close around my throat as he slammed me against the wall, each one digging in deeper than the next. The young man was strong, more so than I had anticipated. "Their instructions were to hold your group, comfortably of course, but as a warning to get your friends under control. I had been told that there were other criminals being hanged today, apart from that group. I didn't find out that a mistake had been made until it was too late."

"Liar! How could you do this to me? I've done nothing but give you my loyalty from the first day I walked into this place." I felt the spittle from his mouth sting my face, and I wished I could wipe it from my skin.

Poor, naïve boy. Though he appeared sure, I saw a little change in his eyes, one that told me his tough veneer had cracked ever so slightly, just enough to exploit. He was breaking, and I would crawl into the broken parts, not only to save myself from being choked to death but to keep an ally from becoming an enemy.

"Ford, you have been nothing but good to me and this town. Why would I want to punish you? I swear to you it was a tragic mistake. I cannot tell you how very sorry I am. The people who made such a huge error are now in the cell where your parents were, and there they will remain. I will allow you to do with them as you wish; whatever you need to feel some relief from the pain you are in."

"Why would you have had them in there at all in the first place?"

"It was for their protection. Until the others were dealt with, I had to make sure they weren't seen. Then, they were going to be moved to a comfortable and secure location. I was going to reveal that I had them at the right time…the time that would have the most impact on your friends' behavior." I sighed. "Those people who you were with before here…they want to destroy this place. They want to burn down everything we've built. Riley…even she can't be trusted." I gazed at him with the eyes that I imagined a loving father figure would have. I wondered if I had gone too far, mentioning the girl, but he seemed to still be engaged. I chose my next words carefully. "Tell me, you've never trusted Cain Foley, correct? Despite what anyone told you? Trust me, Son, you were right all along. He's been a fugitive for years, killed more people than I can count. He even left me for dead many years ago. Your judgement was sound. Those who made you try to doubt yourself are the ones that you can't rely on. Even Riley's too far gone. She's been under his spell for far too long."

He released me, but his eyes were once again hard as stone.

"What about Riley?"

"She was seen running away from the warehouse a while back. Her friend caused a distraction, so she could sneak out, but one of my guards saw her and the priest running away. They haven't earned the right to know what's in that warehouse. If that place were to be compromised, all would be lost. There's something in there that's going to help solve our population problem, something to give us a way to relocate people to other safe villages so we don't have to turn anyone away."

There's a trick to releasing just the right information at just the right time, and I had mastered it. I cautiously put my hands on his shoulders. "As I said, we were going to keep your families comfortable but keep them contained nonetheless, as a warning. Believe me, I wish we hadn't had to resort to such measures, but between that and Cain's history, I had to do something. I admit to you, Ford, that I don't have all the answers. Perhaps it wasn't the best approach, but drastic action had to be taken so they would listen. I have this village to protect. Cain has the ability to ruin everything he touches, has since he was young. He's been one of the most wanted criminals in the world since he was fifteen years old. When other teenage boys were trying to get girls' phone numbers, he was killing people."

I put my arm around his shoulders and guided him to the window overlooking the village. There were only a few twinkling lights left on. The rest of the houses were dark, the residents sound asleep in the security that I provided. They slept the way children slept, without a care in the world, and that was thanks to me. I wondered if they truly appreciated the care it took to keep the place going. Our guards kept the crime rate low, and I had to assume the citizens of my small kingdom were smart enough to know what they had, and the severe consequences if they let their gratitude slip away.

"Why didn't you just kick him out then?"

"Claire. She knows her daughter is attached to him, and if he were gone, Riley would be too." I let my words sink in for a moment. "I was trying to keep Claire happy by having him remain here. I thought I could rein him in—get him to see the value of what we were building together here. The things we do for love, right?"

He didn't say anything, but I knew he agreed with the sentiment. From the way he treated Riley, I could guess that he'd done a few things to win her attention that he wasn't proud of. "Rebuilding the world takes great sacrifice. No life is worth giving up this place…none."

The cracks in Ford's armor of grief were starting

to grow. I could practically watch it split apart within his eyes. Good little workers always believe what you tell them to, especially ones like Ford who I could tell were aching for approval, for just one pat on the back. Anyone could tell the boy was in love, and the object of his affection did not feel the same way. He needed to matter to someone, and I knew I could make myself that person. Craft a good enough story and even the smartest ones drink it in like sweet syrup.

"You still killed my parents, General…"

I sighed deeply, as any guilt-stricken mentor would. "I put them in a position where they were killed accidentally, that is true—but your friends are the ones who put them in danger in the first place. Cain's parents are long dead, so why would he worry about yours or anyone else's? All he cares about is his own agenda. He and his friends are poking around, trying to create turmoil, while we try to bring order from the chaos. They are ungrateful for everything I have given them, even for using my resources to save Cain's life. There's nothing I can do about that. But, I am sorry. Sorry that their reckless disregard for all we have built brought us to this point. Most of all, I'm sorry this terrible accident has made you conflicted." Turning away briefly, I paused, letting him assume my emotion had overtaken me. "I need you, Ford. You—and all loyal citizens—to help us all prosper. Now more than ever…"

Ford stepped back. "I'm sorry, Sir."

I closed the gap between us and embraced him. "All is forgiven. That is if we can still trust one another. Take a few days. To grieve. Then report to your shift first thing."

He nodded as he stepped toward the door, still facing me. "I'll be there, Sir."

I smiled. "I know you will."

CHAPTER TEN

Cain

There was a vacancy in Jordyn's eyes that made ice shoot through my veins. "Of course, I'm sorry this happened. I would never want this for anyone, especially you. You know that."

She shot up off the floor, knocking Riley over in the process. Riley just stayed where she fell. "No...it's more than that. I should have been there." Her voice shook. "But no...I was with you. By your side, like always." She smiled in the way that people falling over the edge do. "You've wrecked my whole life. I was happy. Finally. And now it's gone." Suddenly she started beating me with her fists. I didn't try to stop her. "Thanks to you, McKenzie doesn't have a father. If she's even alive!" Jordyn started to kick toward me too, but Dom grabbed her and pulled her back. In his effort to help me he was hit in the face by a stray elbow several times for his trouble. I felt him looking at me with a mix of pity and sympathy. "The man I

Shattered Night

love is dead and it's your fault! I've wasted my whole life with you, following you around, living your life with you. Maybe I could have been something else, *had* something else, but no...not with you. I would have followed you anywhere. And I did. Devoted sidekick, no matter what the cost. I was your family, and this is what I get." Her voice morphed into a scream. "I should have been with him. If I had been there, this wouldn't have happened. You killed him! Micah is dead because of you!"

I could barely understand her through her tears, but it was enough. She hadn't chosen the life we had, she had just chosen to be my sister. And because of it, she had just had her heart ripped out of her chest, never to be whole again. Everything she said was true. I shouldn't have allowed her to come with us. I should have made her stay behind with her family. I knew Micah couldn't possibly guard all those people by himself, in unfamiliar surroundings. But I was selfish. As I looked down at Riley sitting there on the floor, tears streaming down her face the same as Jordyn's, I realized why. I wanted the woman *I* loved to be protected, and I knew that having Jordyn there with her was the best way to make that happen. She was the only one I trusted to keep Riley safe while I fought off the fever that wanted so badly to overtake me. When death is so close you can touch it, a yearning to save those you love settles in like a cancer. So instead of insisting she stay back with her family, I stayed silent. I put my love before hers, and she would now pay the price for the rest of her days. She had given me her life since we were teenagers and in return, I had taken everything away from her that mattered. "I'm so sorry, Jordyn. I—"

"Save it!" She brought her face right next to mine, and her words softened into a hissed whisper. "We are no longer family. You are no longer my brother." I felt everyone in the room staring at us, the impact of her words floating in the air like a dense fog. When she marched out the door and slammed it shut, no one followed her.

I managed to pull it together long enough to ask the guys to tail her but keep enough distance that she had some privacy. There was still no telling what she would try to do to Keegan if she found him. Olivia volunteered to go too, surprisingly enough sensing that Riley and I needed to be alone.

Once everyone had left, I sank to the floor next to Riley. "What have I done?"

She reached for my hand. I tried to pull it away, but she only gripped it tighter. "It's not your fault. She's just upset. She didn't mean it, I promise."

"Don't try to make excuses for me. She's right. It *is* my fault," I snapped.

"I know you believe that now, but it's not. The only person we can blame for this is Keegan."

Suddenly, I noticed her looking toward the floor. Something was off. "What is it?"

"I'm sorry, Cain, but I have to tell you something." Riley's face grew flushed, that moment before she knew she was about to rain devastation upon me and wished more than anything that she didn't have to.

"What is it?"

Shattered Night

She took a deep breath. "The other people, the ones that were on the platform with Micah...it was the rest of our group. Except for McKenzie and Xander...they're dead. Ford's parents, Reagan's, Natalie...they're all dead."

I could barely breathe. "No...No! That can't be." I got up and kicked one of the dressers that Jordyn had already knocked over. "He couldn't have found all of them...maybe he just found Micah out on a supply run or something."

"Cain...I saw the bodies myself. They're gone. Ford's parents, Reagan's, Jordyn's mom...they're all gone."

I felt something inside me break in two. The people in our group who depended on us the most, the ones that we'd promised to protect...they were gone. We had watched as Keegan snuffed the life out of them, watched as they struggled for their last breath as it slowly slipped away from them and didn't even attempt to stop it as their worlds turned black.

We had failed.

There's nothing quite like dedicating your life to something, only to realize that it didn't work. We had six dead bodies to prove that, and for all we knew, Xander and McKenzie could be two more.

But I didn't have time to think about that, because as we sat there, the bedroom door opened to reveal Keegan standing on the other side.

Flanked by two guards I hadn't seen before, Keegan waltzed in and hovered above us. With a sigh, the poison started flowing. "It seems you've found out. My apologies. I had only meant to contain them. For now. Well, at least that's what I told your friend Ford. The man will believe just about anything." He grinned. "Or maybe that just works for me. What about you, Riley, he's clearly in love with you. Does he behave for you if you lie to him?"

"You son of a bitch!" Riley rose to her feet.

"Keegan, what do you want? They did literally nothing to you. You could have just killed me. I'm the one you really want so why don't you just get on with it?" Riley put a defensive arm across me.

Keegan stepped closer. "Do you remember what you did to me? Do you? Or have you killed so many people that the earliest ones all just blur together? You took my family from me, and now I will take yours, piece by piece, as you watch. And if you try to run? I'll just wipe you all out at once."

"I didn't kill your brother, Keegan. Maureen did."

"Well, unfortunately for you, you picked the wrong team. And let's not forget that you left me for dead on top of it. I almost died because of you. Though, from the looks of what happens to other people who find themselves in your circle, I should count myself lucky to still be breathing at all."

"So you're just going to keep us here? That's your big, elaborate plan? Keep us then kill us off one by one? Somehow I don't think my mother would appreciate that," Riley said as she glared at him.

Keegan laughed the kind of laugh that someone does when they know they have the upper hand. "Oh, you'll tell your mother whatever I want you to

Shattered Night

tell her. Of course, we won't make it obvious. Maybe one of you takes a fall or maybe one of you gets assaulted by an unruly citizen. I'll leave you till last, Riley…" He glanced at Cain and smiled. "…well, second to last, at least, until your mother has worn out her usefulness too. And if you don't comply?" He looked at one of his guards, who cocked his gun. "Well, I'm all for the quick and dirty method too."

"You're even more of a monster than I thought."

He grinned. "It's all in how you look at it, dear. To these people, I'm their liberator, the person who saved them from wandering deserted towns looking for their next meal." He stepped closer to us. "To you, I'm the one who is going to destroy you, one at a time." He squatted down to face us. "Oh, and might want to see where your little friend Nick is tonight. I didn't appreciate him distracting my guards while you ran out of the warehouse. So when he mouthed off earlier this evening, I just couldn't help myself." He reached over and stroked Riley's hair, and she swatted him away as the color drained from her face.

As he and his guards headed toward the door, she ran after him, tugging at the back of his shirt. "No! It was me! Take me instead! No please!" The guard on the right swatted her with the butt of his gun and she fell to the floor.

Before he shut the door, Keegan looked straight at me. "Have a good night."

By the time she regained consciousness, I already had her in my arms. "Cain, it's my fault. It's all my fault. Everything. All of it."

I gently held her as she lay with her head in my lap. "No, I promise you it's not. You did what you had to do to get us the information we needed. Don't blame yourself."

As I held her, Dom, Olivia, Jordyn, and Reagan ran in to find us on the floor. "Oh my God, Cain they took Nick! They threatened to take Jordyn but Nick stepped between them." Dom said.

"We know. Keegan was just here." I couldn't help but notice Jordyn still wasn't looking at me.

"What are we going to do?" Olivia asked.

"I…I don't know."

Now, Jordyn stared at me with a gaze that could ignite a fire. "Why are you confused? We kill him, that's what we do."

"Of course, but we need to get help and get out of here first. We can't let him use those helicopters. We just can't."

"I don't give a damn about the helicopters. He killed Micah." She glanced at Dom. "If he had let me I would have killed him with my bare hands tonight."

I carefully walked toward her but she stepped back. "I'm so sorry, Jordyn, but we can't yet. If Keegan gets control…everyone who lives in America will be in danger. There's no telling how many more people will lose the ones they love."

"The one I care about the most is already dead!" She shouted.

Riley stepped between us. "Believe me, Jordyn, no one disagrees with you. We just want to do this right so no one else has to die."

Jordyn grew silent for quite a while, staring at

Shattered Night

some far beyond place we couldn't see, and probably didn't want to. "Ok. I'll help. I won't kill him—at least not yet." She turned to me. "But after that, I'm done. I want nothing more to do with this. Clear?"

I swallowed hard, realizing that my sister was saying goodbye forever, and forgiveness was not going to be on the table this time. "Clear."

"What are we going to do about Nick? There's no telling what they are going to do to him in there." Dom asked, sitting on one of the beds with his face in his hands. Seeing his large frame bent in half struck fear into my heart in a way very few things could. He'd known Nick longer than any of us. To him, Nick was still the ten-year-old little boy that always gave him the longest hug after Bible study. None of us wanted to think about what may be happening to him, but I knew the unknown was hurting Dom most of all.

And it devastated me that I didn't have an answer.

I decided it best that Riley tell Jordyn that her mother was gone too. So as we left the room, I nodded at her, knowing she would instinctively understand. I didn't want to devastate Jordyn even more than she already was, but I knew that no matter how long we waited, her mother would still be gone, and we couldn't risk Keegan deciding he wanted to be the one to tell her for his own amusement. No amount of stalling would make it any easier to know she was never coming home again.

Or maybe I had let Riley tell her for another

reason; a reason less pretty. Maybe I let Riley do it because I couldn't bear to do it myself. I had already killed Jordyn's spirit that night. Her husband was dead because of a decision I made, and because she loved me as blood. I was too much of a coward to face the fact that her devotion to me had resulted in putting someone she loved in the ground for a second time.

CHAPTER ELEVEN

Nick

The cool, damp air of the jail cell seemed to grab on to every square inch of my lungs, letting a rasping mist overtake them. As much as I tried to get my breath, it was as though every inhale wasn't good enough, and I was left wanting more. I sat in the corner of the room, in a small crevice between the bed and the corner of the wall, holding my knees to my chest to concentrate on doing something, anything really. The jail was made of concrete, and I felt as if I had been tossed into a box that may just serve as my grave. Ford's back was to me as he stood guard outside my cell. "How can you still be working for them? What are you thinking?" I had been in that cell for a week, and I hadn't spoken to him till that moment. I'd rather have stuck to conversation with the occasional mouse that wandered in at my feet, but I had to know how someone we trusted, who knew what Keegan had done, could still be standing there, keeping me from my freedom. He'd lost something too, but it didn't seem to have changed his mind about the guy he called General. "They killed them. Every last one of them. And you're still sucking Keegan's—"

"Shut up. You don't know anything." A second guard walked passed Ford and they nodded at each other, two little maggots slithering past one another in the dark.

"I know enough." I tossed a pebble I found on the ground back and forth between my hands, resisting the temptation to throw it at the traitor's head. "I know that you're either blind or stupid, neither of which is going to help us with jack shit."

Finally, he turned to face me. "I love her. You know that right?"

A laugh burst out of me. "Who? Riley? You have a funny way of showing it. Your definition must be a little skewed."

He grabbed the bars and shook them violently. There was no one else around but his brazen action still shocked me. "It was supposed to be me. Me and her." His voice softened to a whisper. "But I never had a chance. It's always been him. Always will be." He stared up at a small window that was just above the row of cells. "We were just supposed to have a normal life here. She deserved a normal life. She loves him and all he does is keep her surrounded by violence and garbage."

Slowly, he slipped his hand through the bars. After looking over his shoulders, he opened his hand to reveal a key. "Doesn't mean I love her any less though."

Shattered Night

I hesitated, frozen.

"They haven't made me hurt you yet, but they will. I promise, they will. Go up the back stairs. That will lead you to the back of the building where you can slip out without being seen. There's a supply run going out tomorrow. Just hide in the back of one of the cars and get out when the time is right. Stay out of sight in the meantime." He stared at me. "Go get help. Do whatever you need to do but come back here ready for a war."

I still stared at him, waiting for the catch to be revealed. I had never particularly liked Ford, but suddenly the guy who seemed to always be no more than a meat-packed, soft-spoken puppy dog was saving the whole day. I'd seen a lot of strange things traveling the world, but most of the time people were exactly what they appeared to be.

Not today.

"Don't just stand there. You're going to have to choke me. I'll say you caught me distracted, choked me out and took my keys. Oh, and one more thing." He reached for something he had tucked in the back of his jeans, and pulled out Cain's and Riley's knives, handing them to me. "You kind of suck at hiding things. I found these on a sweep before my partner did. Saved them before he saw." I took them gratefully and tucked them safely into the waistband of my own pants. When I was finished, he turned and pressed the back of his neck on top of two of the bars, giving my hands access. I placed them around his waiting throat.

His body twisted as he fell, and for a brief moment, I could see his face. I could have sworn that just as his world went black and he fell to the floor, I saw him smile.

CHAPTER TWELVE

Riley

The sirens woke me from a sleep brought on by mental exhaustion. It'd been a week since we'd seen Nick, and the guards would tell us nothing. He could be dead, vermin crunching on his bones in some rotting prison cell. But when I heard that glorious wail, I knew he was alright. Jordyn knew it too. "Nick?"

"Must be." We quickly dressed then hurried to the guys' room, several other people's doors beginning to open as we passed carefully.

Dom ushered us in. "They're searching the village—must be Nick, right?"

I nodded. "He isn't in here with you, is he?"

Just then it was our turn. The door opened to reveal Ford on the other side. "Nick escaped. Choked me out and took my keys."

Olivia glared at him. "You deserve way worse, you know."

When I looked at Ford's face, I noticed

something I hadn't seen in a long time. As he shyly broke eye contact, I said, "You helped him, didn't you?"

Before he answered, he looked out the door to make sure there weren't any more guards around who could overhear us. "Listen to me. All of you. The General—Keegan does not like to be beaten. He's going to be on high alert now more than ever, and he's going to be coming for all of you. You have to leave. Tonight." He grabbed my hands and his felt cold against my own. "I'm sorry, Riley, for everything." With a kiss on my forehead, he turned to Cain. "The guard that is supposed to be in front of Keegan's bedroom door is choked out in a closet down the hall from his room." He reached into his pocket and handed me a key. "I grabbed this from him before I left him there. The rest of you stay here and wait. If they see most of you it will take them a minute to realize a couple of you are missing. When you go in, look for the internal drawings of all the buildings here. He keeps the only copy hidden in there somewhere. I don't know where, but if you find it, it may help you beat him."

His words hit me right in the gut. I realized what he was doing. "You're saying goodbye, aren't you? You aren't coming with us."

Even Cain protested. "Ford, he's going to know you helped us. You have to come. He'll kill you. You know that."

"I'm going to hide out, don't worry. I'll be all right. I did learn a few things from you guys about staying out of sight. You are going to need all the help you can get. If I'm here, I can help buy you

Shattered Night

some time, and keep my ears open for any information that may be valuable." He handed Cain the gun in his waist holster, then reached down to his leg and took out one from an ankle holster I didn't even know he had. He handed that one to me.

"No! It's too dangerous. I'm not losing anyone else. We can't." I wrapped my arms around him and held on tight, afraid that if I didn't he would slip away, and it really would be the last time I ever saw him.

He returned the gesture and we were silent for what seemed like a long time. Finally, he kissed me on the top of my head one last time and said to Cain, "Take care of her."

"I will." And then Ford did something that I never thought he would. He extended his hand to Cain, and I was able to see one man who despised the other acknowledge that he had lost. Their handshake was slow and deliberate but filled with respect.

As he turned away, Reagan stepped forward. "I'm staying too."

Ford smiled. "No, you're not." He took a deep breath. "Our parents are dead because of him. But he's got a whole lot more resources and manpower than you all do. They're going to need you there to help them win this."

"You're the only family I have left." He seemed almost casual about it, the realization that he was very possibly about to lose his best friend not quite sinking in.

Ford smiled in the somber way that a man does who had resolved himself to his own fate, a certainty of purpose that he may not have liked but knew had to be done. "And you will always be family. Please, I am asking you to go and help protect the thing I love most in the world."

He was looking straight at me.

A look was exchanged between the two men; one filled with history and secrets and love that no one else in the room understood. After the two men embraced for what we were afraid would be the final time, Reagan said, "Ok. I will."

As Ford finally slipped out the door, I fell into Cain's arms, mourning the loss of a friend who was still alive, but likely wouldn't be for much longer.

Sure enough, when we reached Keegan's door, we found it unguarded. We shut the door behind us, and the sirens that were still on covered the click of it swinging against its hinges. "Let's do this quickly and get out of here," Cain said.

"Agreed."

I looked around Keegan's bedroom, a place where I had never imagined I'd be. His four-post bed sat as the focal point of the room, thick and imposing. From what Ford had told me, I realized every little thing, every longing look, every smile I had seen between my mother and Keegan had been a lie. As I stared at the bed, the horror that my mother must have gone through these past months sunk in, and I could barely carry the weight of it. The things she had to do…had to pretend to *want* to do to keep her act believable made a wave of nausea sweep over me like a flood. In my mind, I whispered two words to her over and over again: *I'm sorry.*

Shattered Night

We went through his drawers as quickly and carefully as we could, looking for anything that may hold a secret compartment. We tried our best to put things back where we found them as we went, hoping that he would not realize we had found anything of value or had even been there at all. If he didn't know what we had, he wouldn't have a chance to alter anything.

That is, if we ever found anything worth stealing. I had just gone through the last drawer, and come up empty-handed. "It's not here…I don't see it anywhere."

"Me neither." Cain had just knelt down to look around the floor to see if there was a loose board when we heard something. With the sirens going, we didn't have time to react and found ourselves frozen in place.

When I heard the door shut behind me, I knew it was over.

Except it wasn't. I turned around to see not Keegan as I had expected, but my mother standing before us.

"Riley! Cain! What are you doing in here? Keegan's going to be back here any minute. If he catches you, it's over." She frantically looked behind her, as if the feeling I had deep in my gut moments earlier had leaped into her. There was a tone in her voice that had been missing for a while. It was assertive, in control, and certainly not afraid of telling me what to do.

She shoved something into my hand and pushed me toward the window. I opened my palm to reveal a key with a red rubber covering around the base.

The number "32" was written in black permanent marker. "What's this?"

"It's the key to a back exit in the perimeter wall toward the rear of town that very few people know about. It's only there in case we ever get overrun. The higher-ups can slip out undetected. Look for a bunch of brush that's thicker in one spot than everywhere else. The door is behind it. Get everyone out of here tonight."

I ignored her request. "Why did you pretend to be on Keegan's side? Why didn't you tell me?"

She grabbed me by the shoulders and looked at me right in the eyes. "I will always be on your side, Riley. Always. Never doubt that. I became close to him originally so I could learn all I could until I was able to escape, assuming that you had received my letter. Then you showed up, and I knew something had gone wrong. Yes, I tried to separate you from Cain," she looked over at him, "and I'm not proud of it. But I thought maybe, just maybe, if I could say everything I could think of, hit every nerve that I knew would hurt you, that you would leave this place and never return." She paused. "I'd lose you forever if it meant keeping you safe, and you having a chance at the life you deserve. I love you enough to let you despise me." Looking at me, then Cain, she said, "I'm sorry."

"It's ok, Claire," Cain said.

"But why are you with Keegan? Why are you helping him?"

"When my plan clearly didn't work, and you stayed closer to Cain than ever, my best option was to stay close to Keegan, and maybe I could keep

Shattered Night

you safe." She paused. "Then he killed Micah, Natalie…all of them, and I realized it's only a matter of time before he gets you too."

"We need the schematics of the village."

Claire smirked. "I guarantee you they're in the one spot where you didn't think to look."

"Where?"

Quickly, she went over to Keegan's nightstand and pulled a large Bible off his shelf. But as she opened it, she revealed that it wasn't a Bible at all. Inside of it were several folded up pieces of paper with drawings of buildings on them. "Here. These drawings will give you the information you need. I'll stall them, but you need to get out of here. I'll tell everyone else where to meet you."

"But you have to come with us."

"She's right, Claire. If he finds out you helped us, then you're in terrible danger." Cain begged her with his eyes, as did I.

She smiled. "Well, then he better not find out. I'll be more help here."

"Please, Mom."

She put her hands on my shoulders. "Bo went back all those years ago so that we could be safe. Now it's my turn to stay behind. Go!"

With tears in my eyes, I slid open the window. "I love you, Mom."

"I love you too." I was halfway outside when she spoke again, with a venom in her voice that I didn't know she was capable of. "And Riley? When you come back, kill him…kill them all."

Luckily, there was a balcony right under Keegan's room to lessen the distance we had to fall.

Once we landed there, we dropped the rest of the way down, landing safely on the ground below. "You go meet everyone at the gate. There's something else we have to do before we leave.

Cain shook his head. "No way. We aren't separating."

"We have to."

"Why?"

"Because we need Adam. Without him, we don't have reinforcements, at least not until Nick gets back." I didn't tell Cain the last part of my thought: *if he gets back*.

Cain looked as if he were about to protest but didn't. Instead, he said, "We go together and meet up with everyone after. Which way?"

When we reached the outside of Adam's place, the door was open. I could see shadows dancing on the walls in the candlelight.

He wasn't alone.

"I'm telling you, I don't know!" I heard Adam's voice, followed by a loud thud.

"Come on, you don't think we don't know about your little band of rebels? And I do mean little. We just let you pretend to be secretive so we can monitor you. If you so much as looked at any of us the wrong way, we could have snuffed you out a long time ago."

"I don't know what you are talking about."

The guard laughed. "Oh really? So it won't bother you to know that the rest of your pathetic little group is sitting in a jail cell right now? Thomas, Maggie, Roland…all of them. The only thing that's keeping them from being executed is that we had a massive one such a short time ago. All we need is a little distance, then they're next."

Silence. My head felt tingly as I realized that our numbers would be even smaller than we had thought. There would be no teaching Adam's people how to fight. The only battle that they could be a part of would be staying alive long enough for us to set them free.

"That's what I thought. Just a matter of time…tick-tock, tick-tock. After all that the General has done for you. Some people just aren't happy with anything. They take and they take and they take, but what do they contribute? Nothing." The guard clutched one of Adam's plants in his thick fingers and tore it from its pot. "You don't think we could get someone else to do this job in about ten minutes? We don't need you. So, you best behave yourself." We listened carefully to his ramblings as we snuck ever closer to him, keeping cover behind the many plants that Adam tended to. His tone was cold, so much like how I had imagined Keegan sounded before his rebirth as General Cole.

And he had no idea what was coming.

The man didn't hear Cain come up behind him. By the time he realized there were hands around his throat, it was too late, and he slipped into unconsciousness, the plant that he had ruined falling from his hand. "Adam, we have to go," I said.

"Why do I have a feeling you guys are somehow responsible for these damn sirens?" He turned to Cain. "And who is this?"

"He's—"

"Wait, he's him, isn't he? I don't know why I

even asked." He held out his hand. "Glad to finally meet you."

"Likewise."

"Adam, we have to get out of here. They've figured out Nick escaped. Once they figure out he's long gone, they're going to come after us. And you." I looked at the man on the floor. "Looks like they already have."

"I can't just leave my people behind." He shook his head.

"There's nothing you can do for them right now," Cain said. "The best chance they have is for us to bring these people down before they do another mass execution. No matter what's going on, that guard was right. They can't do another one, not yet. Your people are safe for now. But their time is running out."

"Cain's right. Coming with us is the best way to help them."

Adam ran his hand across his workbench and looked around at his handiwork. Every plant was perfectly pruned, every fruit without a blemish on it. Though we knew how he felt about the governing system there, he seemed to care about his own piece of that place. "You work so hard to make a life, only to find out it's not what you thought. Sometimes I wish I could just live in the illusion like so many of the other people here. It would be easier.

"Yes, but it wouldn't be real," Cain said.

"Sometimes, reality is overrated."

I couldn't argue with him there.

Adam came with us to the gate where we met up

with the rest of our group. Mom was right. There was no one there guarding it. It seemed almost too easy, and I found myself waiting for someone to jump out from some hiding spot and expose us all. But having a secret gate fit Keegan. When it came down to it, he would make sure he had an exit strategy for himself that wouldn't be interfered with by other people. I smiled to myself, realizing that his selfishness was what had allowed us to have an exit strategy. Once he realized it, maybe he would rethink his emergency backup plan.

I wondered if he had actually told my mother about it, or if she had just overheard him talking. I knew that Keegan was the kind of man who would save himself, and leave my mother to whatever fate had in store for her. My limbs felt weak as I thought about what was going to happen to my mother when he figured out we were gone. I tried to push the thought away, but a vision of her with a rope around her neck kept appearing in my mind, making me shut my eyes tight in an attempt to erase it. Yet, as soon as it went away, it reappeared again, each time more terrifying than the next. I wondered if I would have a chance to thank her again, and to apologize for everything I'd ever done, thought, or said against her. I shook away the realization that there were too many times to count.

If she dies, I will never forgive myself.

"So, now what? We're out…we're weaponless…and outnumbered. Any bright ideas?" Jordyn asked. "Oh, I *still* didn't get my gun back."

Cain spoke. "For now, let's all find somewhere to get some rest."

"I heard some of the locals talking about an abandoned neighborhood nearby. If we pick a house in the middle and guard in shifts, we should be ok temporarily. I think it's in this direction," Reagan gestured toward our right and behind us.

"Sounds good." We all followed in line behind Reagan and Cain. We stepped as lightly as we could, just in case there were any of Keegan's men out for a late-night patrol. We didn't need any trouble…there would be plenty coming our way quickly. The night reminded me of my first fighting lesson with Cain, or as he had told me, my first taste of learning how to pay attention to everything around me: every sound, every smell, every shift in the wind. I knew that naïve, sheltered teenage girl was gone forever, but I was proud of the warrior standing in her place. I hoped Cain was too.

The neighborhood reminded me of Hannah and Charlie's, the one we stayed in on our first journey out of America, the adventure that brought Cain into my life for the first time. For a split second, I could imagine children playing tag in the front yard of one, or a woman sitting on the porch of another. I could imagine the crisp white paint under the dirt and overgrowth. It looked like it was a place that made people very happy long ago, but the empty holster at my waist reminded me that time had passed, and it may never be that peaceful again.

We looked at the supplies we had brought, all quickly thrown into bags on our way out. They were minuscule, mostly just snacks we had saved from the cafeteria, and blankets from our beds. I was mostly thankful that I had taken extra water bottles every time Keegan wasn't looking and had thought to stuff them into the bags along with our granola bars and fruit snacks. Each of us had a bottle of water and a breakfast bar, but it wasn't nearly enough to chase off the hunger.

***

We kept moving for two months, sleeping in a new place each night and laying low. After much thought, we decided that the best thing to do would be to keep moving but stay nearby, assuming that Keegan would think we would be trying to get as far away from his place as possible. There were plenty of empty stores and abandoned homes for us to hide in, and we took full advantage. In the hopes that Nick could find his way back to us, we left little clues giving him hints that we were out of the village, and to try and find us. We also used that time to send pairs of us back in, hoping to learn everything we could about the layout of the village and what we were up against, stealing food when we could as we tried to figure out what to do next. We all knew we had a battle to fight…we just didn't know how we could possibly win.

We were just settling into our guard shift one evening when we heard a rustling outside. My stomach turned, and I was afraid our revolution would be snuffed out before it had even begun until I heard a familiar voice. "Riley! Cain! What the hell are you guys doing out here?"

I looked up to see Nick's bright orange hair glowing in the moonlight at the base of the porch of the house we were staying in. I got up and gave him a welcomed hug. "Nick! Oh, my gosh, I was so worried."

When I released him, Cain had his turn. "So good to see you, man. How did you find us?" He smiled mischievously. "Did you get my messages?"

"We've been around for a while, trying to figure out the best way to get to you guys, when I started to notice that there was a Bible verse on a piece of paper in every single house we slept in. Didn't make sense, not with every house being ransacked for years. Something like that wouldn't have been left out in the open, not that many times." He snickered and smiled at Cain. "I had a suspicion it was you, but when I saw "…the house of the righteous shall stand," I knew for sure. We must have all picked the same shelters, since, you know, you trained me and all. I figured you guys got out and had the same plan we did, stay out of sight and keep moving. Only a matter of time before we ran into each other."

"I knew you'd pick up on that." He patted Nick on the back. "Well done."

I looked at Nick. "We? Who's we?"

"You can come out now."

I glanced behind him to see Verita emerge from the darkness. Without a word, we looked at each other, and all that had happened before was forgotten. I held her tight. "I thought I was never going to see you again."

"You were right, Riley. You were right about everything. Sophie did get Cain shot. I'm so sorry." Her tears glistened.

Shattered Night

"Don't you be sorry. She's the one who did that, not you. I'm so happy you're here!"

"I was on my way to find you when I saw Nick coming toward me heading in the opposite direction. He filled me in on what's been going on." Everyone else got up and greeted her. After her last hug, she looked back at the faces in the group. "Wait a second. Where's Ford? And your mom?"

My face burned. "They're still inside. Mom stayed so we could get out and have some time to get away. Ford...Ford's still there too."

Nick put a hand on my shoulder. "He's the one who helped me escape. Don't worry, he's not lost to us yet."

"I hate to break up a good reunion, but there's still business to get to here. What the hell's the plan?" Olivia said as she, Dom, Jordyn, and Reagan emerged from the house. She burrowed under Reagan's arm when she was finished scolding us.

Cain nodded. "She's right. We have to figure out how to take control from Keegan. If we don't put a stop to him, he's going to spread his power all over the country. He's going to poison everything, and there may not be a way to undo it if it gets that far. We have to stop him now."

"But there's still the issue of numbers," Adam said.

Nick grinned. "Not anymore." He nodded at Verita.

"You can come out too," she yelled behind her. As she did so, several people emerged from the trees, as if they had come straight out of the earth. They all looked around our age, and it only took

Cain a moment to recognize them.

They were his originals.

The New Underground Railroad, the system that had become the Guide Network, had all started with one van full of delinquent children who were escaping from life on the street, prison, or worse. These were those children. Nyla, Maynard, Alexis…all of them had come back when they heard their leader was in danger. Nick smiled. "They're why I was gone for a bit. Had to wait for reinforcements. I put out a call through the Guide Network. When they heard you needed help, none of them thought twice."

"Not a blink between them," Verita said.

I squeezed Cain's hand. "These are them?" I nodded at the new group. "I feel like…I feel like I already know you. You've been alive in his stories for years. And now here you are."

"Oh, and one more thing," Nick said as he pulled off his pack and sat it on the ground. "I thought you may want these back." He extended his hands and presented myself and Cain with our knives. "Ford gave them to me before I escaped. You two were a little out of sorts without them."

I grabbed mine gratefully, cradling it gently in the palm of my hand. "You did it. I was afraid to think it was possible, but you did it. Thank you. I don't think you get it—giving these back, bringing them here—doesn't just give us weapons, it gives us hope." He put his arm around me, and as we watched Cain with the others, I hoped he grasped just how important he was to all of us.

Like they did when they were small, the entire

group of originals threw their arms around Cain at once, and he did the same. He tried to wipe the tears from his cheeks before anyone saw, but I did, and I suspected others did too. Gently, he tore each person away from the group, hugging them individually and asking them how they were doing, and of course, thanking them for leaving their own lives behind to dive into something incredibly dangerous with us. "With your help, I know we can beat him."

Dominic took his turn as well. "I cannot tell you how much it warms my heart to have you all together again. If this can happen, anything can. I can't believe how blessed we are to all be here under the same moon tonight. Truly, this is amazing."

Verita and Nick informed us that there was an abandoned church about a half mile back from where they came from. "If we stay in the basements where the supply storage was, and have guard shifts, we should be ok. There's less chance of us getting caught there than if we stay in the neighborhood. And if needed, it's surrounded by trees, so there were plenty of places to run.

I hoped we wouldn't need to.

As I watched all of us settle in, I thought about how fitting it was that our journey would end where it all began. Cain had started the Guide system in a church basement, and a church basement was where we would gather to finish what he began so many years ago. Surrounded by boxes, firewood, and cans of food, I smiled as I looked around at the familiar faces, as well as the ones who were brand new to me. I watched Cain and saw him in a way I had only imagined before, as he commanded the role of the father he had never had so perfectly. Even Jordyn, who hadn't said much more than a couple words to him, smiled as she watched him laugh at jokes from years ago and listen with the attention of a teacher. For a brief moment, I imagined us in a small home, out in the country, with a child, playing outside in the day and sitting on Cain's knee listening to stories at night before bed. But as my hand brushed against the knife at my hip, the image faded away.

For quite a while, there was no talk of war or the death that we knew was coming. Old friends smiled at each other and talked of fond memories and moments that they thought no one else could recall. We passed around water from our supplies, and all drank from the same jug pretending it was the finest wine. I thought about everything it took to get to that moment: escaping America, the downfall of a country, the crumbling of a world. One twist in circumstance and it all would have been different. Dominic came up to me as I watched from the sidelines. "Taking it all in, huh?" I asked.

"Something like that. Feels like something's coming, doesn't it? The calm before the storm."

I sighed. "Something like that."

Dominic handed me the water. "Well, here's to a fine tornado."

I raised the bottle. "Cheers."

Finally, Adam spoke. "Look, I appreciate that you are all glad to be back together after all these years, but I have people still inside." He looked at me. "As do some of you all. Now that we have more people to fight, we need to figure out what to do and we need to act now. Who knows if the people inside are hurt or worse…"

Silence filled the air with the realization of the inevitable. "He's right," Cain turned to Nick and gently put his hands on the younger man's shoulders. "I appreciate everything you've done. You have no idea how much it means to me. But, even having all of us here, it's still not enough. There's just too many of them, too many men and too many guns. We need to figure out something else."

Nick grinned. "Cain, you're back. That's all we need. You're well again, that's what matters." He sighed deeply, looking with admiration at the man who had changed his life forever. "We would follow you to the ends of the earth, you know that. You saved us. You believed in us. Please, let us believe in you."

Before Cain could respond, another voice joined the conversation. "They have way more weapons than we do. If we don't have the element of surprise, we have nothing," Nyla, one of Cain's originals, said.

There was a sudden crack as Maynard whipped open his switchblade. "Weapons aren't much of an advantage when the lights go out. I'll slip in there and cut the power. Nick told us there's only power in certain areas."

"Excellent." Nick smiled, but then silence filled the room once again. We'd gotten step one, but it seemed no one had any idea about step two…until a voice I didn't expect rose from the quiet.

"What's the thing they are most concerned about in there?" Olivia asked.

"Those helicopters, of course. Why?" Jordyn looked at her.

"Because we need to blow them up.'"

Jordyn smiled. "Well, I don't think we have the supplies for an explosion but we can sure set some shit on fire."

The two women grinned at each other.

"But remember," Cain said, "*If* we go in, this is about a regime change. We are not going in there to take as many casualties as possible..." He looked at Jordyn, "though some of us may have every reason to. The only one who has to die is Keegan. Of course, protect yourselves first, but only take life, if you must. Once their leader is gone, my bet is most of those people in there will fall in line."

"What if they don't?" Adam asked.

Cain hesitated. "We will deal with it on a person-by-person basis."

The rest of the night was spent grouping everyone up. Cain let Nick take the lead and lingered in the background as the rest of us discussed our plan. I wondered why he wasn't taking more of an active role but assumed he agreed with what we were doing since he didn't say otherwise. Nick's optimism had an effect...I personally felt lighter after he had spoken about what was to come.

Maynard would cut the power, with Nick covering his back. As much as we all wanted to set some fires, we thought that would draw too much attention. A power outage could be blamed on a mechanical malfunction, where a fire had more potential to alert them to human presence. Dom, Jordyn, and Reagan would partner up to capture as many of Keegan's men as they could, while Cain and I would find Keegan himself. Olivia would have one of the most important jobs of all: finding my mom and getting her to safety while the rest of us were doing our jobs.

"But, Riley, I don't even know how to fight."

I tucked a loose strand of hair behind her ear, as my mother used to do for me. "You're smart. And fierce. If I had to bet on anyone getting my mother out of this if something goes wrong, it'd be you."

Olivia swallowed hard, and, for the first time in a long time, hugged me. Though she always seemed so sure of herself, I was suspicious that most of it was for show. After my compliment touched her so deeply, I knew I was right.

After everyone was satisfied with our plan, while the rest were turning in, I went outside to get some air, when I heard yelling from behind the church. When I rounded the corner, I saw Cain and Nick, both with reddened faces and anger in their voices.

"How can you even say that? You really don't believe in us anymore, do you? We were all willing to come here, to possibly lay down our lives because you said we couldn't let this go on. We cannot leave Keegan in power. You are our leader. So stop being a pussy and lead us! We need to get this done now!"

"Sometimes being a good leader means knowing when to retreat," Cain said. There was a growl in his voice, a primal desperation that made my breath catch in my throat.

"What the hell is going on?"

Nick turned to me. "Cain doesn't think we should attack. He wants to wait around till some magical second option drops in our lap. By that time more people will be dead."

"*We* are the ones who will be dead if we do this. I'm not willing to risk all of your lives by bringing knives to a gun fight! The price is just too high. I'm tired of losing people to fight some cause. Let someone else take him down. I can't stomach losing one more person because of that bastard."

I stepped between them. "Cain, why didn't you say anything when we were coming up with the plan?"

He paused, running his hands through his hair, and pulling out the little toy soldier that he always carried with him, the one he'd had since he'd left America ten years earlier, from the shopkeeper who made their escape possible. "Because I don't know what to do instead. Riley, I'm lost. I don't want it to be our fight anymore, but I don't know who else can take him down or would want to. Everyone in that place has been sucked into his orbit, and he has a damn good plan of how to make his orbit bigger. Keegan needs to go, but I have no idea how to win this without many of us dying in the process. None."

I grabbed his hand and held it in my own. "Yes you do. Together. We win when we're together. And inside that building is everyone that loves you. We've conquered everything that's come at us

Shattered Night

before. You'll see. Just have faith in us, the same as we have in you."

Nick slapped him on the back. "You aren't going to talk us out of this. Riley's right. We've faced impossible odds before, and because of you, we've made it out the other side. We've got you. We've all got you."

As the stars looked down at us, there was a sadness in Cain's eyes as he embraced me. "I know."

Later that evening, Cain and I were about to crawl under our blanket when Jordyn came up behind us. "Could I talk to you? Alone?" She was looking at Cain.

"Of course."

They left me huddled on top of a blanket and found a darkened corner of the basement. It was about as alone as they were going to get in a room stuffed with people. But we all had the decency to pretend we couldn't hear them.

"I didn't mean it. What I said."

"Yes…you did. And I get it."

"Ok, maybe I did right that very second, when I said it. But I didn't mean it for real."

I couldn't resist. I peeked up from my blanket to see Jordyn, my tough, stern Jordyn, looking down at the floor, moving a pebble around with her toe. "You were grieving. You will always be grieving," Cain said. "I get it."

"But, we might die. And soon. I'm still mad at you but I just want you to know that I didn't mean it, not really. You didn't kill him, *he* did. You've always been my family and you always will be. I love you…asshole." With tears sliding down her cheeks, glistening in the small amount of light we had in the basement, she threw her arms around the man who she loved most in the world.

"I love you too."

I smiled to myself as I turned away from them, listening to the soft whisper of voices and sleeping breaths around me.

CHAPTER THIRTEEN

Keegan

Claire had tea waiting for me when I got back to my room...*our* room. It was sitting on the dresser, steam pouring hauntingly into the air. The sirens had finally been turned off, but there was still a wailing in my head. "You shouldn't have," I said.

She went over to it and handed me the cup. "I thought it might help you sleep after all this commotion." Her smile was pleasant enough. But as her words came out, I wondered if she knew it was over for her. "After you're done, we should really get to bed."

I stared at her, taking a cautious sip. If I hadn't seen her coming out of my office with my own eyes, I wouldn't have believed it. When I saw that the emergency gate key was missing, that's when I knew for sure: Claire had betrayed me. "Yes, we should." I continued to look at her, and she turned away from the weight of my stare, avoiding my eyes by finding things in the room to straighten up.

As she fiddled with the clothes in her drawer, folded blankets, and straightened pillows, she asked, "Did you find the missing prisoner?"

"You wonder if it would have been better for everyone if you'd never existed, don't you?" I said declaratively, not as a question. I already knew the answer.

She froze, hands lingering on top of the blanket we had on the foot of the bed. "Excuse me?"

I walked toward her, slowly, methodically. "It's true. I get it. If I were in your position I'd be wondering the same thing." I sat the empty teacup on the bed and approached her from behind. "Perhaps they would have been. Everything was a mess before you stuck your nose in it, there's no question about that. But at least children knew where they were going to sleep at night. Who knows where they ended up after you were finished with them?"

"You bastard."

As I looked down at her, I saw her chin tremble. I leaned in and whispered in her ear. "And what about Riley? She would have never met Cain at all. Someone like her would probably be on her way to marrying some dull but sweet, hardworking man with a decent job who could provide for the grandchildren you'll never have."

She scurried away from me. "Why are you doing this? Why are you saying these awful things?"

"Do they hurt because I'm saying them, or do they hurt because they are true?"

"You're being cruel."

"So a bit of both then." She moved quickly

around our room, keeping her back to me, and I could tell the pieces of what was about to happen were starting to fit together. "Tell me, what do you think they are going to find when they come back for you? Did you think you would still be standing?" I placed each of my hands on either side of the wall, pinning her to it. "Or do you think they will come back at all? They do seem to love a good cause. Maybe they will pick it over you, and tonight was the last time you will see them."

Tears ran down her cheeks, dampening her shirt, but I laughed. "It really would be justice, wouldn't it? You did single-handedly destroy everything, after all. Maybe you should go down with the ship. A good captain always does."

"You're the one who wrecked everything. You and your people. You twisted the law into something ugly. You twisted it and twisted it until it was a mangled form of what it was supposed to be. All those families that were torn apart, that's on you, not me."

"You sure about that?"

She turned around and stared at me, silently. I already knew the answer to my question. "Whatever you're going to do, get on with it then. Spare me the theatrics." Her words were tough, but the strength melted away under the weight of the tears streaming down her face.

I put my hand on her shoulder and she shoved it away. Immediately after she did so, I placed it back where it was. This time, she left it there. "We could have done great things together, you and me. We did. But you wrecked it, just like you do to everything you touch. Maybe after I throw you in a cell, I'll toss in a rope. Or a pill. I'll give you a way out, Claire, so you can save your precious daughter the trouble of pretending for a moment longer that you aren't the thing that made the world come crashing down."

I didn't need to put handcuffs on her. We walked to the jail, and as I threw her inside, I gave her one last kiss on the cheek. She didn't look at me, and I knew she was broken.

CHAPTER FOURTEEN

Cain

I woke up in the middle of the night, the heaviness of what we were going to do eating away at my mind. I had tried to talk Nick down, but he was stubborn, and that resolve seemed to have slipped into the rest of our group. Perhaps they were right. I did think that there was a possibility we could win, but there would be a heavy price to pay for that victory. It was a mathematical certainty that not all of us would make it out alive. If we even lost one more person, that was too many. But if I didn't come up with a better idea, and soon, that was exactly what was going to happen. Someone would die, and the question of who it would be was the only one that remained.

I got up slowly, not wanting to wake Riley, when I noticed Dom sitting in the corner of the church basement, looking at something by flashlight. As I got closer, I realized it wasn't a Bible as I had suspected, but something else. "Who is that?" I asked as the photo came into view. A sad smile spread across his face, but he didn't look up from the picture. "My sister. Serena."

"Dom, I had no idea. Where is she now?"

"Gone. Died years ago. She was just seventeen, gunned down by some man who wanted the ten dollars she had in her purse." He paused, and I noticed there was a tear threatening to slide down his cheek. "That's what sent me over the edge, why I ended up in prison." He held her photo carefully between his fingers, gently enough to make sure he didn't wrinkle it.

I put my hand on his shoulder. "Dom, why didn't you tell me? I'm so sorry." Not only was I sorry he had never told me, I was torn up that I had never bothered to ask.

It was then that he looked up at me. "I hurt people, Cain. People who just happen to get in my way. I never brought it up because I didn't want to." He gently slid the photo back into his Bible. "Get up. Get up and walk with me. I have something to show you."

We disappeared into the woods near the church, and the silence that I would normally find comforting felt suffocating. The woods were usually a place for me to come and feel safe, but knowing what we were planning to do, I started to wonder if I would ever feel safe again.

After walking for several minutes, I almost tripped over it.

"Look..." Dom pointed at the soil near my feet. It seemed uneven as if it had been disturbed recently. I had seen dirt in that state before, more times than I would like to remember, yet recalled every second of every time exactly. This was the sign of an unmarked grave.

And as I gazed up, I saw several more plots with dirt lain down in the exact same manner, stretched out for several yards in front of us, so far that we lost the edge of them in the trees.

"I would have to assume that these are the graves of all the people Keegan and his men have killed, either by execution or by so-called accidents," Dom said.

"There must be dozens of them."

"Exactly."

I hesitated before I spoke, reluctant to acknowledge the thought that I was sure was playing in both our minds. "Micah, Natalie, and Ford and Reagan's parents…they are probably buried somewhere here."

"I would imagine so. Though, I am surprised a man like Keegan wouldn't just burn them."

I knew why. "It's just another way to get back at me. Bury the people we love in the woods, alone, with no marker to call their own. The same as Maureen and I did to his brother, his family. He probably hoped we would somehow find them like this, nameless, as if they never walked the earth at all." I shook my head. "God, we were just kids then. All we knew was we didn't want to go to jail. We both knew even though the guy was awful, he had a family somewhere. That one thing set all of this in motion. Maybe this is what I deserve."

"What?"

"Knowing that this is all my fault."

Dominic forcefully turned me around to face him. "No! This is Keegan's fault, not yours. You were just trying to help someone you cared about. And now this psychopath is on the verge of doing what he tried to do to you to the rest of the country…try to pull them in with compliments and sugary words and if it doesn't work, take what he wants, no matter what the cost." He paused, gesturing to the graves stretched before us. "Back then, when Serena died, I fought, but not the right fight. My grief took the form of beatings and violence on people who just had the misfortune of looking at me the wrong way. I took my anger out on anyone that happened to cross my path. That's why I swore I'd never fight again. Your fight isn't like that. Yours has a purpose. This is why I brought you out here. To see this…to remind you what we're fighting for. This is what this man is capable of, and it's going to take a special kind of enemy to beat him. It's going to take you."

His words touched me, but there was still a weight bearing down on my chest. "Dom, I'm so tired. Just so tired."

He embraced me. "I know, Son. I know."

We headed back to the church and with the smells and sounds of the forest surrounding us, I wondered how it all would end, and I prayed that the man that I thought of as a father would get the ending he deserved: a home, a bed, and a safe place to live the way he saw fit. If I didn't make it, I didn't want my death to destroy him in the way I was afraid it would. I ached to know that even if he lost me, his faith in the God that he had dedicated his life to would remain steadfast, and he would still be able to pass the comfort of it along to other children, in the way he had given it to me. If I discovered the fight that was coming would be my final one, knowing he would continue being a leader and healer would help me face my last moments with a smile in my heart. And as I thought about the field of death that moments ago laid before us, I realized that there was a good chance that this battle would, in fact, be my last, and I would have to leave the woman and the family that I loved so deeply to continue on without me…if the fight didn't take them right alongside me. There's nothing quite like knowing that through no choice of your own, you would possibly have to hand the responsibility of caring for the person you loved the most over to someone else. But even as I thought it, I knew it wasn't true. I did have a choice. There was always a choice. I could go back to the church, take Riley's hand, and tear her away from the madness we called our lives. We could live in a little house somewhere, isolated, and safe, ever able to feel our love for each other until we grew old side-by-side.

But neither of us could live with that. That's the ironic part of morality. Those without a moral compass have no trouble taking the selfish road, and are rewarded with a long, happy life, where those who are plagued by a conscious, the knowledge that they could fix a wrong in the world, tend to lose themselves in the process of saving others, and must part ways with the happiness that they have clearly earned, but would ever be just out of reach.

As the church came into view, I saw Olivia

running toward us with panic in her eyes. "Oh thank God. Come quick. Jordyn's lost it."

I barely heard our feet hit the ground as we followed.

When we got to the front of the church, we saw a crowd once again surrounding a few people in the center of it. One was Jordyn, one was Nick, and two were wearing Keegan's guard uniforms.

The guards were screaming.

As Dom and I pushed our way through, we heard Jordyn's voice above the others. "Oh, you want me to stop? Is that what you said?" I got there in time to see two men tied to separate chairs, and her pulling one's head back by his hair. "I really wished you'd stopped a while back too. Back when you helped that son of a bitch hang my family."

"We weren't even there! We were guarding the food storage at the other end of the village."

"Yeah! We didn't even know about it until it was all over!" echoed the other man.

Suddenly, Jordyn let out a giggle that I'd never heard before, the kind that usually precedes slipping into madness. "But you were there! Your complacency was there. Your support was there. Don't you see that if he didn't have all of you he wouldn't be able to do the things that he does?" She inched closer to the second man. "Don't you see? It *is* your fault. Almost as much as his. And if I can't have him, I'll take you…"

"Stop!" I yelled as she squeezed her hands around the man's throat.

"Oh hello, Cain. Look, I got you some hostages. Heard them chatting rather loudly as they were

Shattered Night

coming back toward the village. Seems they got a little off course." She didn't let go.

"Jordyn, these men didn't kill Micah. Please stop." I hoped she would loosen her grip but she didn't. The man was starting to turn blue, and I knew if I didn't get her away from him we would have a dead body on our hands. Forcefully, I removed Jordyn's hands from around his throat. The man gasped for air and coughed with the effort.

What have I done to her?

"I'm sorry, Cain, we were on patrol…I couldn't stop her, so I grabbed the second one when she grabbed the first so he couldn't run away," Nick said.

"You did the right thing, but now we have to figure out how to clean up the mess we're in."

Jordyn laughed, insanity seeping off the sound. "Mess? What mess? They're disposable." She begged me. "You wouldn't let me have Keegan. Let me have this. Please."

I pulled her aside, away from the crowd. "Jordyn, you know I know what it's like to kill someone who didn't deserve it. These men don't deserve it. They're like Ford, just caught up in a world of lies and bullshit, and now they can't get out of it. They couldn't leave Keegan's army if they wanted to.

"Cain…please…"

"Jordyn…"

"I've never asked you for anything, have I? Not once."

As desperately as she thought she needed to kill those men, I knew how much pain still hung in my heart years later after killing Bo. I didn't want that for her. But I did have to admit to myself, a deep, almost buried part, that I wondered if it was my decision to make. "We will keep them inside the church until we figure this out. Let. Them. Go."

With a cold stare, she nodded. She walked back to the men and started untying the binds of one, as Nick started untying the other. I told Nick and a few others to usher them inside and re-secure them safely inside. I desperately hoped Jordyn would thank me later, but even if she didn't, I was determined to do right by her, even if it meant she may hate me for the rest of our lives. I let out a sigh of relief as I watched the two men start to walk toward the church.

I noticed the edge of the gun she was using for patrol peeking out of her jeans a second too late. As she got to the edge of the crowd and drew it out, I got to her just in time to hear her say, "Run, little sheep, run," as she pulled the trigger, not once, but twice. As the men's bodies hit the ground, I knew that the Jordyn I loved may be lost forever.

For a moment, I just stood there, silently, as did everyone else. "We were just checking the area to make sure they were alone. What have you done?" I heard Verita say to Jordyn, with Riley at her side. "Keegan's going to be furious. You just upped our timeframe on a situation that we are already not prepared for!"

Though I knew she was right, my instinct to protect my sister kicked in. "He was already mad." I turned to Nick, Verita, and Riley. "You guys, please take her inside. Dom, please help me get rid of the bodies. Maybe he will think they just got held back on whatever mission they were on." Even as I said the words I knew they weren't true.

As everyone filed inside, I looked at Dom. "Did she just destroy this whole thing?"

He sighed. "I don't know."

"Maybe we should all just run. I mean God, Dom, now we killed two of his people. He's going to be extra motivated to capture all of us and do God knows what." I sucked in a breath as my imagination went to work. "I can't bear to think what he is doing to Claire right now."

"Then we better make sure we're ready to win."

"I don't even know where anyone's heads are at after today. I don't know if I can or should ask any of them to lay down their lives for a cause that all of them believe in based on my word alone."

"You didn't ask in the first place. They wanted to be here. They heard you were in trouble and they dropped everything to come help and risk their lives in the process. He grabbed the legs of the first man. "Now come on, we have work to do."

CHAPTER FIFTEEN

Riley

The following evening, we were ready–as ready as we were going to be. Our numbers were still incredibly small. But we knew we could fight. When the lights went out, we would be equipped, and they would not. We just hoped that would be enough.

It had to be.

We didn't want to risk leaving the basement in case there were some of Keegan's men in the area, so I snuggled close to Cain. "What do you think our chances are?"

"Honestly, I don't know." He stared at me. "But I know one thing. I've always known it."

"What's that?"

He rose from our spot and got down on one knee. "That I am totally, utterly, and hopelessly in love with you. I don't want to spend one more minute without you as my wife. Riley, will you marry me?"

Shattered Night

I heard the crowd around us clapping, cheers echoing around us, but all I could see was him. "Yes! Of course I will!"

He embraced me, and we kissed for what seemed like seconds and forever at the same time. "I wish I had a ring for you."

"That's ok, I—"

"You do." Jordyn emerged from the back of the crowd. The look on her face was somber but sure. She took the ring off her own hand and handed it to Cain. "Until our circumstances are different…"

"Oh God, Jordyn I can't."

"No, Jordyn, this isn't right," Cain agreed and tried to hand the ring back to her, but she wouldn't take it. Instead, she pulled another ring out of her pocket: Micah's. After I had pulled it off his hand so she wouldn't see, I had waited until she was calm to give it to her. At the time, it seemed to offer comfort, something left of him that wasn't buried forever.

"I want you to have this. He…he would want you to have this."

Cain couldn't look at her. "I can't. You know I can't."

"Please. I need you to have this. Someone needs to have their forever. I need someone to be ok. You need to do this for me. *I* need to do this for me."

Cain swallowed hard and closed his eyes for just a second too long, a second that let me know he was trying not to cry for his sister, for Micah, and for everything we'd lost. "Ok."

Though she had insisted on giving us the rings, after she had, she stoically slipped back toward the back of the crowd. I ached to go after her, to comfort her, but I knew nothing I could say would ever be enough. So optimistically, selfishly, I let what was about to happen continue. I'm not proud of it, and I probably never will be. But I knew that for one or both of us there might not be an after the battle. I had one chance to get what I'd wanted for so long, and I took it.

Father Dominic came over and put a hand on each of our shoulders. "I would be honored if—"

"Was there ever even a question?" Cain and I both smiled.

Under the stars of what we both knew may be our last night together, Cain and I vowed to love each other. We didn't need to…it was already decided long ago. But with our family around us, we said the words anyway. Though it was the happiest night of my life, there was someone missing, and the thought of it made my heart ache. Cain knew without me having to say it. "Your mom would want you to have this moment, right here. Especially now. She'd want you to relish in it and hold onto it tightly."

I kissed him. "I know." I *did* know. But yet the ache remained.

Father Dominic interrupted us. "I hate to do this to you, but you know I have to. This is a happy occasion, but we still have a battle ahead of us." He gestured to the group before us and turned to Cain. "I think they need to hear from their leader." I stepped back, along with Dom. With his protective arm around me, we watched.

Cain looked around at the familiar faces, ones

that had changed with time and space. They were bathed in the moonlight, and given the strong, sure adults I saw, I imagined he could only see traces of the scared children that he had met so long ago, children that had changed his life forever. They were brought together again by what on the surface seemed to be Keegan, but I knew better...we all did. All I had to do was study the awed expressions that covered the room to know the truth. It was their love for Cain and their gratitude for the freedom that he had risked his life to give them.

"Tomorrow, we fight. By the cover of night, we will take control back from a man who has taken so much from us. But not just for ourselves. We fight for those who can't...those who don't even know what's coming."

We felt the fear radiating off the crowd, yet there was something else too: resolve. He'd helped these kids survive, and while he had lived for them, they were now willing to possibly die for him. "We've faced him before...and we've won." He threw his fist into the air with the force of generals who came before him. "And we will again!" His soldiers cheered, thrusting their weapons to the ceiling, and Cain watched as knives, guns, and arrows twinkled against the starlight that streamed in through the small, dusty window. He paced the room, looking at everyone who would fight beside him.

"They dismissed us, all of us. The country we were born in threw us away, telling us we were nothing, not worthy of hope, not worthy of understanding, and not worthy of love. But from the gutter, surrounded by darkness, we will rise, and save those who cannot save themselves. Who knew that it would be the warriors of the underground, the ones they forced to live in the shadows, who would save them all! Tomorrow, we will tell Keegan that we are the soul of the night, and we will be his reckoning!"

Jordyn caught his eye, and with the simplest nod, she told him one last time that she would stand beside him in every sense of the word. This would be another battle that they would fight together, like every one before it.

About an hour later, everyone was preparing for what was about to happen in their own way. Some were reading, some were thinking, and some talked to each other about nothing…and about anything. Cain noticed Dom was reading a small Bible that he always kept in his back pocket, staring somberly at the pages. We sat down beside him. "What's wrong? Other than the obvious?" Cain asked. The only person who had ever truly been a father to him was sitting on the floor in the dark, squinting desperately so he could read the words he found most precious.

Dom smiled a sad smile, closed his Bible, and put it back in his pocket. Though he seemed willing to do so, I felt as if we had violated him somehow, interrupting something that he valued with his whole heart, right when he needed it most. "I haven't done this in so long, and I swore I would never do it again."

"What?" I asked.

"Fight." His expression was heavy and he stared out at the sleeping people around him, who, to him, would always be children. "I swore after I became a priest, I would never again lift a finger in violence against another man."

Cain put a hand on his shoulder. "I am sorry, Dom. Truly. But tomorrow, we need the convict, not the preacher."

He smiled again. "Maybe you need both."

Around two o'clock in the morning, Cain had everyone ready at the front of the church. I will never forget the feeling of anticipation hovering in the air, like static in the dark. The contrast of the scene was not lost on any of us, a pure white church hovering over us as we set out on a quest for blood. Suddenly, in the midst of our preparing, Cain looked at Jordyn. "Jordyn, I need you to come with me for a second." I looked at him, confused at what could be so important that he had to call her away just as we were about to confront Keegan and his men.

"Why?" She asked, apparently as confused as I was.

"Just come with me." She hesitated, then followed him back into the church basement.

Ten minutes later, I heard yelling. Afraid they would alert someone to our location, I broke away from the group and found them. It was then that I saw Jordyn with her hands cuffed behind her back, and Nick standing next to them, "What the hell is going on?"

Nick addressed Jordyn. "I'm sorry."

"Jordyn, you know you are in no state to fight today. You are grieving, and I won't have you getting yourself killed. I couldn't bear it," Cain said.

"You? Why the fuck is it always about you? What about what I need?" She spit toward him. But a mere second after she did it, her expression turned to desperation. "Please, Cain, I need to do this. You can't take this from me!" Her face was red and frantic tears splashed into the dirt at her feet. Sweat glistened on her brow as she begged him for the opportunity to get the vengeance she desperately needed and even more desperately deserved.

"Jordyn, I'm so sorry. I never wanted any of this for you." He could barely look at her. "If I could take it back, if I could take all of it back, I would. I would even wish that I'd never met you so I wouldn't have had a chance to drag you down this path to Hell right alongside me. But I won't let you do this."

"Cain…" I looked at him. "Cain, she's right. You can't do this to her."

He stared at me as I emerged from behind them. "What?"

"If you do this she's never going to be able to heal."

"How do you know that?"

I sighed, recalling the silent promise I had made to myself weeks earlier. If Keegan took Cain from me, I would take vengeance, and never have a moment's peace until I had. "Because I would feel the same way if what happened to Micah happened to you."

He begged me with his eyes. "She's not ready for something this big. Riley, she'll get herself killed. You know that. I can't bear the weight of losing any more of the people we love."

Shattered Night

"And if we do, my heart will be breaking right alongside yours."

He hesitated for a moment, then I saw his face change into something that I'd never seen before, at least not directed at me: rage, and a frustration from years of fighting other people's battles settling on him with a crushing weight. "If she dies, that's on you." He nodded at Nick, and as Nick slid the key into the cuffs, I wondered if something had just shifted between me and Cain forever, and the thought of it made a panicked tingling sensation sweep over me. It was a sensation I'd felt several times before, when I'd had a knife aimed at me. But this time there was no knife, only him.

We were approaching the edge of the village under the stars that seemed to twinkle just a little brighter. I wasn't sure if it was encouragement, or their attempt to illuminate us for our enemies. Once we saw the lights go out and the smoke billowing from the warehouse, we were going to head in.

Cain hadn't spoken to me since I made him release Jordyn. "Shouldn't we at least talk about this?"

"Later."

"But, Cain, I—"

He turned to me. "Later."

I was about to protest when the village went black. Dominic looked at us. "It's time."

We started heading toward the village, under the cover of darkness. It grew steadily in the distance. I looked for that familiar feeling inside me, the one I had every single time before when I had gotten into a fight with Cain at my side. I was used to us moving as one, like we shared the same breath, the same lungs.

Something was missing.

I can't be sure if I first noticed his footsteps weren't beside me, or if I just stopped feeling his presence all together, but suddenly, a pain filled my gut, one that I'd only felt once before, when the boat that was supposed to have carried Cain back to me was empty, bobbing lightly against the shore.

I looked around me, studying a sea of faces, but only looking for one. They were steadfast and sure, but as their resolve grew, mine crumbled. "Where is he? Dom, where is he?"

Dom looked around, and as he couldn't find the one face he wanted to see either, his quick glances in all directions became frantic, desperate. "I…I don't know. He wouldn't have…"

I hadn't known where to go, what to do, shivering as the wave of familiar uncertainty that I hadn't felt since Rome washed back over me. But there was one thing I was sure of.

Our battle was over.

As quickly as I could, I ran to the front of the crowd, whipping around and facing our group. "Stop! Everyone, stop! We can't do this!"

Jordyn was the first one to reach me. "What are you talking about? We can't back out now."

"We have to."

"Why?"

I inhaled deeply and said the words that, until that moment, I had been certain I would never have to say again, the words he'd promised I'd never have to. "It's Cain. He's gone."

CHAPTER SIXTEEN

Cain

I wasn't sure exactly what I was going to say, but I knew what I had to do. My legs felt heavy as I made my way back toward the entrance of the village. Our group had been heading toward the back, so they wouldn't see me as I walked right toward the main entrance. This wasn't the first time I had gone to turn myself in to Keegan. But this time would be a little different. Because I was certain, especially after so much time, he would not make the same mistake twice.

Once I went through those doors, I was nearly certain that I wasn't walking out.

I cursed myself as I went, remembering what the last conversation I had with Riley was. There was a distinct possibility that the last words I spoke to the woman I love were *not* that she meant everything to me, that she had somehow found her way into every single piece of my soul. Instead, they were full of anger, and misplaced anger at that. Riley was not to blame for anything that happened to Jordyn that night. What was about to happen to the people I loved was on me and me alone.

And there may never be a chance to tell her I'm sorry.

I came up to the night guards with my arms raised. Even though I did not present a threat, they drew their guns. "I'm here to see Keegan…I mean, General Cole."

The guards looked at each other. "Name?"

"Cain Foley."

This time, one guard radioed in. I could hear part of the conversation. "I understand, Sir. I'll bring him up immediately." He looked at the other guard. "This is him. We're supposed to take him up."

One stood in front of me with his gun aimed at my head, while the other put handcuffs on my wrists behind my back. "Come with us."

Some of the villagers tried to pretend they weren't curious, giving their plants water with empty watering cans in the middle of the night so they could see what mysterious stranger was being led toward their leader's home. As I walked, I thought about everyone I was leaving behind, who maybe, just maybe, I could save with one final act. Dom, Nick…they were willing to die for me, along with everyone else I had been about to lead into a battle that we couldn't win.

And Riley…

Now, any slim hope we'd had of having a normal life together was gone. Even if I was able to escape, I had done the one thing she couldn't recover from—I left her again. She had barely been able to forgive me the first time. Even if I could make it back to her, we could never truly go back to how we were. More than likely though, she would become a wife and a widow in a matter of hours.

Perhaps it was better that way.

More than anything, more than my own life, I wanted to save her, and if meeting with Keegan one-on-one could make that happen, it was a chance I was more than willing to take. She had been cursed with the burden of loving me, and perhaps after I was gone she would be able to find someone who could give her what I could not. Maybe she would have children someday, the normal life that for us seemed forever out of our grasp. The thought of it gave me peace and made me sick all at once. It was supposed to be her and I growing old at each other's sides.

But maybe what I wanted and what she needed were two different things.

I tried to savor the sweet aroma of the night air as I was lead inside, holding onto the smell of baking bread and smoking meats mixed with cool grass and a warm, misty rain. But as the door shut behind us, I was greeted with ammonia and lemon instead, chemical fumes that let me know if Keegan wanted to wipe me out of existence, he could do so in an instant, and there wouldn't even be a body left to find.

They took me to a room that was apparently Keegan's office. He was sitting at a mahogany desk with his back to me and turned around in his chair when he heard the door open. I noticed a fireplace in the corner and a brown leather sofa directly across from the desk. "Un-cuff him."

"Sir, are you sure?"

"Do it."

My wrists ached as one of the guards released me. "I'm here to turn myself in."

"Are you now?"

Ironically, the man with the power stayed sitting, while I, a man who had probably just sentenced himself to die, stood tall. "Yes. You know you've just wanted me this whole time. Now you have me. Just kill me like you want to and leave the rest alone. This can all be over. You can have your show, and they can have their lives."

"What about your little cause? I won't be giving up my helicopters any time soon. I know you found out about them."

I sighed. "Someone else will have to find a way to beat you. You aren't invincible, Keegan. Someone will figure out where the crack in your armor is, but it won't be me. Too many of my people have died already."

Keegan leaned forward in his chair. "Now, what makes you think I won't just kill you, then send my men out to slaughter all your little friends?"

"Because I have the one thing you want that you have no other way to get."

"And what's that?"

"I'm the only one on this earth who can tell you where your brother is buried."

Silence. He and I stared at each other for a long moment, then he said, "You're really willing to die for them? But why would you think they wouldn't make some ill-fated rescue attempt?"

Shattered Night

My eyes narrowed. "Because I deserted them, the one thing they never expected me to do." As we spoke, I remembered the last conversation I had with Claire, and felt a wave of understanding wash over me. "I left because I love them enough to let them hate me." The words stuck in my throat. "Have you ever loved someone that much?"

Keegan didn't answer, just rubbed his chin as he stared into his fireplace. In another life, maybe he would have told me the truth. Instead, I got nothing. "Very well. What do you propose?"

"You give them safe passage abroad, the further away from here the better. When I get word that they are all safe, I will tell you where your brother is. Then, you can do with me what you will."

"And if they won't leave?"

"Tell them I made a deal with you, for all our safety."

"At the expense of your cause?"

I hesitated. "Yes."

Keegan grinned. "You will take me to my brother, yes. But I'm going to require a little insurance." He faced his guards. "Take a group of men. Find our missing guests, and when you do, lock them up tight."

I lunged toward him. "No! You just wanted me!"

"You're going to give me what I want. You and I are going to take a little trip. And if you don't deliver, my men are going to hang your friends in the town square, and they can join the rest of your people in the ground."

When we got to the rear entrance of the village, there was one of his infamous helicopters waiting for us, with a man who I assumed was a pilot waiting next to it. I let out a deep breath when I looked around and saw no one and noticed there were no screams of capture echoing in the night. Our group was nowhere to be found. As I suspected, once they figured out their leader had abandoned them, the battle had stopped before it began.

He shoved me into the back passenger seat, and the hinges squealed as he shut the door. I looked around and saw that he had installed a barrier between us and the pilot, similar to that of a limousine. "What is this?"

"I thought we could have a little alone time. A friendly little road trip if you will." Though his tone was casual, he took out a set of handcuffs from his pocket. "But, put these back on."

We sat in silence for quite a while. I looked out the window, noticing the lights of the village slowly fade away. As we flew, I saw a scattering of other lights along the way, but not nearly as many as there were in Keegan's domain. If something went wrong, there wasn't anyone around for my friends to run to. It would be a long road to find help if they even made it that far.

I noticed the weight of something pushing against my seat. It wasn't heavy enough to be a lot of weaponry, so I guessed it was a supply pack. "Sure you brought enough supplies? I'm not going to be much use to you if you let me starve."

"I'm sure. And I know who to punish when we get back if I'm wrong."

Quiet fell upon us once again. As the hours

Shattered Night

passed, I hoped that, eventually, Keegan would fall asleep, and that would give me a few precious minutes alone where I could look in the supplies and see exactly what I was dealing with. But that thought was fleeting. He would never let his guard down, which meant the contents of that bag would be unknown to me until they were out in the open.

"Do you miss her?"

His question confused me. "Riley? What do you think?"

"Maureen."

"Don't say her name. You don't get to say her name." Hearing it cross his lips made my muscles tense.

"So you do miss her then...how sweet. Miss Riley must not be the jealous type."

I steadied myself, willing myself to stay calm. "No, I don't miss her. But that doesn't mean I don't care that she was taken away from this world way too soon and that I'm sitting next to the person responsible. And that doesn't mean you get to say her name." After a long pause, I said. "Do you miss your brother?"

"Not really." His answer surprised me. Not the words themselves, but when I glanced over at him, I could tell that he meant them, or at least thought he did.

"You don't miss him, yet you've been after me for protecting his killer for years. Why are we doing this then? There has to be something, some semblance of feeling there."

Keegan laughed darkly, and the sound made me shiver. "There's no such feeling. I didn't much care for him when he was alive—he was a bit of a sniveling idiot, always causing problems. But he was family. *My* family. And when someone harms your family, you have a responsibility to make it right, no matter how you felt about the particular individual. Wouldn't you agree?"

Much to my dismay, I did. Well, I would agree had I grown up under normal, white-picket-fence-type circumstances. I thought back to whom my blood relatives were, and realized there were only two people I would consider actually putting that into practice for: my grandparents. If someone had harmed my mother, I couldn't see myself doing much about it. And my father…I had snuffed his life out myself.

"We're entering the D.C. border." He looked at me. "Home sweet home."

"Good…now tell the pilot to turn around."

"Don't fuck with me."

"I'm not. You don't think we would have buried him in the city limits, do you? Turn around and there's a back road a few miles from here. Have him land this thing in the woods wherever is flat enough. Then we are going to go back to where the pavement turns to dirt, so I can retrace my steps." After a moment's hesitation, Keegan repeated my instructions to the pilot. As he landed, and we emerged from the helicopter, his face seemed to change. "Even when we find the end of the road, exactly are you going to remember where he is? It's been so long and everywhere around here looks the same…why I'd imagine you picked it in the first place. How are we going to find him?"

Shattered Night

"If you ever trust me on one thing, trust me on this. You don't forget something like that. Even for someone like me, you don't forget the first time you put a corpse into the ground. Never." He looked for a moment as if he was going to argue but didn't. I wondered if he was remembering the first time he had to dispose of his own kill, or perhaps he'd never had to do such dirty work, always finding someone else to do it for him. He followed me back toward where we had seen the road from the window.

After we found the end of the road, he pushed me forward. "Walk." Contrary to my nature, I did what I was told. As we went, I tried to push away the flashes of memory that plagued my mind's eye: lifeless flesh, dirt under my fingernails, Maureen's face covered with mud.

We hiked a couple miles inward when I saw it. "He's here." I pointed to a triangle of trees. "We put him toward the far right of this triangle."

He pointed to the ground. "Make sure."

"We don't have a shovel with us."

At that time, I finally got to see the first item that was in his mysterious pack. Without a word, he tossed me a small trowel, something more appropriate for planting bulbs than digging graves. It landed heavily at my feet, and I knew what he had in mind. The flight alone with him was not going to be the only punishment I would endure. I would be forced to undo my mistake, both figuratively and literally. Undoing my handcuffs, he said, "Yes, we do. Get digging."

My skin burned, and my fingernails were in shards by the time I reached the top of the body's head. As I dug, all I could hear was the sound of the wind whispering through the trees. I looked up at Keegan and started to keep going. "No, that's enough."

He kneeled and unzipped the pack. For a moment, I suspected that his plan was to shoot me dead and leave me buried in an unmarked grave right beside his brother. It would have been fitting. Not the spectacle I'm sure he wanted but fitting nonetheless. But as he unzipped the bag, he didn't pull out a gun, but a small rock gravestone. I watched as cloth draped out of the bag too, something that he must have wrapped the gravestone in to keep it safe. He held it in his hands, and I could barely read the name on the front, with the dates of his birth and death. "Cover him back up."

The entire time I threw dirt back into the hole I had just dug, Keegan squatted down on the ground, staring at the gravestone. "Make sure the dirt is smooth." It was an odd thing. I thought I would be feeling intense anger at that point, after the exhaustion, after the aching hands. But from somewhere deep inside me, I felt a wave of sadness. He was a murderer, psychotic, and had changed the course of my life. But he was also someone's brother and, despite his words, what we were doing was clearly not just about familial obligation. He took a deep breath and got to his feet. When he reached the place where he now knew his brother's head was, he carefully placed the stone in the upright position. "Now. Now it's finished." He didn't say anything else, but when he thought I

Shattered Night

wasn't looking, he gave a slight nod and blew a subtle kiss toward the grave. And under his breath, I may have heard, "Goodbye, little brother. Until I see you again."

Keegan hopped in the front passenger seat when we returned to the helicopter. As we headed back down to the village, I glanced out the back window at Washington, D.C. My life had started there, and there was a part of me who believed it would end there. But that was not to be, because as it disappeared behind us, Keegan, said, "They should have the gallows up by the time we return." He paused. "There won't be a bag over your head. I want everyone to see the face of the war criminal, the terrorist who will finally be brought to justice before their eyes. If you cry out, if you speak at all, someone you love will die. If you speak again, someone else you love will die. And so on and so forth until you become like me: a man alone with nothing left in the world. But don't worry, you won't feel that way for long." And just like that, the protective older brother who had shown himself to me so briefly was gone, leaving only the monster in his place.

When we arrived back at the village, Keegan tossed me in a cell himself. He did it under the cover of night, claiming that he didn't want to spoil the surprise for his fellow citizens. As he threw me to the ground, he said, "Sleep tight. Here in the damp air with the rats where you belong." With that, he winked. "I'll see you soon."

The bed was just a few pieces of plywood, not even a blanket. I was used to sleeping in such uncomfortable places, so I lay down and stared up at the ceiling, letting the drops of condensation gently land on me.

I wondered if Keegan's plans had come to pass as he thought while we were gone. I didn't see or hear anyone else that I knew in any of the cells next to me. I considered he may have them held somewhere else but realized that he would want me to hear them, to know they were there, just out of reach. So, the fact that they weren't told me that maybe, just maybe, they were ok.

With that thought, I finally slept.

CHAPTER SEVENTEEN

Riley

It probably wasn't true, but I felt as if our crowd of supporters was surrounding me like a thick, suffocating fog. None of us knew what to do, and we all stood frozen in the space that was supposed to be the beginning of our charge on the village. My breath quickened, the open space around me closing tighter and tighter.

"What do we do?" a voice said.

"Where the hell did he go?" said another

"Will he come back?" said a third.

I threw my hands on my ears and closed my eyes, trying to give myself a moment to think. I didn't have an answer for any of them and was afraid I never would—until I felt someone rip me out of the cocoon of muffled sound. "Riley, they're coming. You have to listen to me."

I opened my eyes and found someone I hadn't expected to see that night, if ever again. Ford had grabbed me by the shoulders, so tightly that I feared he may leave a mark. "Who's coming?"

"Soldiers."

"What?"

He turned so he could address the whole group. "They're coming to round everyone here up. A group of twenty men. If you don't get ready you're all going to die."

Whispers of panic filled the crowd. "But this wasn't the plan! Why is this happening?"

"Because Cain turned himself in."

My heart dropped. I couldn't speak, but Ford seemed to know what I wanted to say. "I'm sure he didn't tell you because he knew you'd never let him do it."

He was right. And now Cain was gone, along with his and my chance to close the rift between us.

"But we were about to fight!"

"You were about to lose," Ford said. "Now everyone, listen to me carefully. You're going to have to trust me." He sighed. "I know I don't deserve it, but please do it anyway. Get back to the church right now. You can fight them there, on your own turf, and in smaller numbers than you would have otherwise. You know it better than they do, and I'll tell you right now, you're better fighters. They may have guns, but they've never been to war. They've never had to exist in the shadows, or figured out how to not be seen by their enemy. They've never had to. Tonight, they will regret it. *You* can make them." I looked at him, and for a moment, I forgot we were about to face a number of soldiers who doubled our own, and realized I was proud of him. "Now this is where you need to trust

Shattered Night

me. You need to leave some of these guys alive."

I guessed where he was going. "To trade for Cain!"

"But Cain left us," someone said. "For all we know he made a deal with Keegan."

I turned around and figured out the voice belonged to one of the originals, Nyla. I pushed against her chest. "Don't you ever say something like that again, you hear me? If you do I'll have you on the ground faster than you can open that poisonous little mouth."

Jordyn and Verita pulled me away from her. "We don't have time for this. Riley, it's your call," Verita said.

Though it made me uneasy to be thrown into another plan of attack so quickly, I took a deep breath. Ford was right. This was an opportunity and we had to grab it before it slipped away. "All right everyone, this is what we've been ready for our whole lives. Hell, this has *been* our whole lives. You know how to disappear, and you know how to fight. Be patient, be calculating, and we will pick them off one-by-one." I looked around at the people I adored, men and women who had changed me, and those who I loved because they loved the same man as I did, and gave them a smile of a fighter ready to do what she did best. This was our time, and the fate of our country rested on our shoulders. I knew there were no other people in the world that I would rather trust with that burden, all the while wishing that I didn't have to. "And when I give the signal, all hell breaks loose…"

Like a night from what seemed like years ago,

Jordyn, Verita, Ford, and Reagan all nodded at me approvingly, and we all disappeared into the night. But this time, we knew what was coming. This time, *we* would be the ones to attack.

We would fight with a purpose bigger than any of us had before. If we lost, it was over for us, for our world, and for the man we all loved more than ourselves.

***

The soldiers all marched into the clearing in front of the church. They kept a formation until they got to the front door. Two went in the front, while one took the right side, and another took the left. They all emerged from the front at the same time. "They're not here."

"They have to be. This is the most isolated spot for miles. Did you check the basement?"

"Yes, of course I checked the basement."

The commanding officer said, "Fan out, let's check the surrounding area. Remember men, keep your guard up. These aren't just some street rats that are going to roll over the minute they see a gun."

Respect, I thought. I hoped he was one of the ones we kept alive.

The first soldiers faced an arrow through the heart. I couldn't see who fired it, and, as planned, they disappeared into the darkness as quickly as they had come. Another quickly came up to check his pulse. "Dead."

"By who?"

"I don't know, I don't see any—" Another

Shattered Night

arrow, this time through the head.

"Get down!" I heard one voice shout.

"Take cover!" And another, their panic ringing through the night air.

Two were dead, and not one bullet had been fired.

I heard the sound of a man trying to speak after his throat had been slashed coming from near my hiding spot. Again, their assailant was gone before anyone found them. This time another soldier aimed his gun and fired several rounds at nothing but night air and darkness.

They're starting to panic...good.

With their numbers dwindling quickly, the rest of the soldiers made a mistake. They backed themselves together, forming a cluster in the middle of the clearing. I was certain in normal circumstances they would have realized that critical error, but they'd never faced invisible enemies before, and the battle strategy they had arrived with crumbled into dust.

Though the hand on my knife itched to throw it, and the adrenaline that I hadn't felt in a long time returned to my veins, I waited. I stayed still and watched as our young fighters picked off men twice their age, some with arrows, some with well-aimed knives.

When there were only ten left, we emerged from the trees.

I plunged my knife into the chest of the man closest to me before he could even raise his gun. Some of the other soldiers were lucky enough to fire off a couple rounds, but none hit anything.

When there were only five men left, I grabbed one of them and had my knife to his throat. "Everyone hold your fire or this man dies." They must have believed me because they all lowered their guns without question. Nick and Verita collected their weapons, and Verita guarded them far out of reach of any soldier who may have tried to get them back.

We used the soldiers' own zip ties and handcuffs to secure them. "At first light, we get Cain back." I was met with cheers, but Ford pulled me aside.

"Riley, I have a plan. I know you have no reason to trust me, but I'm asking you to anyway. For a second time."

There was a time I would have said no, not that far in the past. But the Ford standing in front of me was different. He'd saved Nick–he'd saved us all. "Ok, Ford. I'm listening."

"Keegan can't be a leader without people to follow him. I know you want to get Cain back, but we also need to take Keegan down before he does what he did to our families to anyone else." He grabbed me by the shoulders and stared at me unblinkingly. "He cannot remain in power." I didn't like where he was heading, but I kept quiet. "Tie me up the same as the rest of them but leave my gag on loose enough that I can get it off at the right moment." He paused. "When we go to make the trade, we need Keegan to decline."

"Um, what? No way in hell. He'll kill Cain."

"Keegan's men need to see that he's willing to sacrifice them for his own power. They need to see that we aren't this big happy family that Keegan pretends we are. We need him to say no, and the other men need to think he's sending our hostages to their death."

"What about Cain?"

"I will convince them to abandon Keegan. We will be able to save Cain in time."

"But what if you can't?"

He looked at me, and where there was jealousy before, there was only pain. "Cain was willing to die to protect the country from a monster. He was willing to throw himself on the sword to save all of you. Please…you have to do this, or all the people we've lost will have been for nothing."

My knees buckled, and I hunched on the ground. I was not willing to sacrifice Cain in the way he had decided, without me, to sacrifice himself. He had done the thing he promised never to do again: he'd left me, deciding what was best for me without my consent. And now he may die for it. I hated him and loved him completely all at once. He'd broken his word, the one thing that he knew would potentially make me turn away, and he did it on purpose. The only thing we had for certain in our world was our own choices, and even that had been taken from me. He did not have the right to try to destroy my love for him, for whatever excuse he conjured up; it was mine and mine alone. He was my everything, and no matter what he did, he always would be. But as much as every fiber in my body was screaming, I knew that even if we did convert all of Keegan's men over to our side, he would be in such close proximity to Cain that he would probably be able to kill him anyway before we could release him. The terrible realization sliced through me as if I had turned my blade on myself.

No matter what I did, Cain was going to die.

***

Ford reached out to a fellow guard who he knew he could trust and found out when exactly Keegan was planning to hang Cain. And with that guard's help, we were able to sneak out the one person who had been missing from our group for so long, the person who could fill the emptiness that I had carried with me since we had climbed out Keegan's window so many nights ago. As my mother ran toward me, the world stopped for the briefest of moments. But as I turned around and saw the soldiers behind me with gags in their mouths, it started moving again, and I fought hard to remain balanced.

We reached the guards at the front of the village by early morning on the day Keegan had chosen for Cain's death. Verita, Reagan, Jordyn, and Nick flanked the hostages, each holding one of the soldier's guns in their hands. As we approached, Maynard emerged from behind some of the tents, having hidden himself in the village after he had cut the power. I gave him a relieved nod as he blended back into our group while we marched.

I had done as Ford had wanted, and tied him up along with the rest, leaving his gag loose for when the time came for him to make his case. We purposely staged adding him to the other group of hostages, putting on a show so the other soldiers wouldn't be suspicious since he hadn't originally been with them.

As we reached the town square, I saw that the gallows had already been prepared. A crowd was gathered, ready for an execution, but none had expected the parade of prisoners that they saw coming toward them. Whispers filled the crowd and I wondered what they were saying about us. But when I looked up at the gallows, I didn't care.

Cain was standing there, with his hands behind his back, a rope around his neck, and Keegan at his side. There were extra ropes there once again, the same as the first time Keegan had taken away people we loved. Perhaps this time he planned on putting those around mine, Jordyn, Dom, and Nick's necks before he took Cain from us so that the last thing he saw would be our deaths at Keegan's hand. I almost buckled, my resolve disintegrating as I watched Keegan tighten his grip on Cain's shoulder. Our hostage parade ended several feet away from the scaffolding. I wanted to force Keegan to leave his post, to get down on our level rather than towering over us, but he remained steadfast. "Let Cain go," I shouted. "We have your men. Six men for one." I paused. "Only one…and you can save their lives."

"My good people, look in front of you. These people have terrorized the men you trust to protect you. These…monsters have tied them up, and marched in here, expecting to make the rules." He gestured toward us. By then, four of his other guards had gathered around him, probably to make sure we didn't come with any surprises. "But terrorists don't make the rules, do they?" I heard whispers of agreement flooding through the crowd, and I felt sick.

I turned around, addressing the people directly. "These are his soldiers, men your leader claims to love as family…as brothers. Are you hearing this? He's willing to sacrifice them to keep one man…to feed his own ego."

Keegan feigned shock. "Ego? This man has been a wanted fugitive for over ten years! He's wanted for acts of terrorism all around the world. I would be doing a disservice to the communities these men have vowed to protect if I were to let him go."

"Yes, I remember him. I read about him years ago. You caught him!" someone said.

"He deserves to hang!" a young woman's voice said. I wondered why we were fighting so hard to protect people who had such a thirst for blood. We were good people…were they? I wasn't sure anymore. But I was sure of one thing—the crowd was turning against us.

I had hoped not to involve her, but I didn't have a choice. This particular battle was going to come down to words, not knives, and I knew just which weapon to bring to that fight. She had single-handedly destroyed a country. Perhaps, this time, her words would bring it back together. "Maybe you can't listen to me, you don't know me. But if you won't believe me, believe *her*."

Our group parted, and my mother emerged from the back. The woman I had remembered from her speeches so many years ago had returned in every way. Her footsteps had changed, the tone of her voice. Every part of her knew our lives depended on

Shattered Night

her and her alone, and every part of her was ready. "You all know me. I've talked with you over dinner. I've held your children's hands while they lay sick in their beds. We've talked about the past and daydreamed about the future. Together. And I understand that future is something that we owe to this man, the person you know as General Cole. He created this village; he and his men have kept us alive." She turned and looked Keegan right in the eyes. "And we are eternally grateful." I waited for Keegan to say something, to stop her, but he seemed as hypnotized as the rest of us, lured in by her compliments and unsuspecting of what would follow. "But what is the cost? What is this community if we find out it's built on the bodies of the ones we love?" Her voice boomed. "The people you've seen take their last breath in this very square, this spot—they were no more criminals than you or I. They were your brothers, sisters, husbands, mothers, those who," she pointed at Keegan, "he deemed worthy for death because they dared utter a dissenting word. Just words. That was supposed to be what made us different, us as Americans. The country as we knew it is gone but that spirit still remains. We are supposed to be the ones who have the freedom to love or despise our government as we so choose." She paused. "If we lose that, we've lost everything."

It was then that Ford revealed himself. "It's true. It's all true. Please, I was one of them. Those last people who you saw die in front of you on this very ground were my parents, and the family of my friends." He fought the tears that threatened to come. "That man took their lives to do nothing more than prove a point. It should be him standing there with a rope around his neck!"

My mother stepped toward the gallows. At first, Keegan's men blocked her, but he waved them off with a flick of his hand. I wasn't sure if he let her come to him out of morbid curiosity or because he still didn't understand that she was a threat. Whatever the reason was though, what she said next changed everything. "You're going to pay for what you did to Bo! You killed a good man you son of a bitch! You'll be sorry!" She turned toward the crowd. "This man, among all his other crimes…he murdered the man who saved my life. He sacrificed himself to save my daughter and me, and for that, this man put a bullet in him. It could have happened to any one of you. And in many cases, it has. Don't let him lead you any longer. No one else that we love has to die."

My stomach fluttered, as if it had flown into my throat.

"Bo? What are you talking about? Bo Dodson?" Keegan asked.

She glared at him. "You don't even remember his name. You've hurt so many people they must just all blur together for you. But no matter, he'll get his justice soon."

Keegan laughed. "I may be responsible for a lot of things, but that's not one of them. Sure, I was going to kill him. But I wanted information first and he was dead when my men got there." He inched closer to her. "You can't blame that one on me."

From the gallows, Cain and I stared at each

Shattered Night

other, panic flowing through my blood.

"You're a liar. Cain told me your men killed him." She looked at Cain. "Cain, he's a liar and a coward. Right? Tell him…"

She noticed the color drain from my face the same time Keegan did. When the pieces fit together, he smiled. "Oh, how interesting…Cain, do you have a little something you want to share with Claire?" He looked at me, and, from the delight on his face, I realized he had figured out my secret as well. "Oh, my! Do *both* of you have something you want to get off your chests? It seems you've been keeping a secret from dear Claire for a very long time."

Keegan had one of his men temporarily let Cain off of the platform, keeping a gun at his back. It was obvious he could see what was about to happen. Our group was about to crumble, and he didn't have to fire a shot. My mother looked at Cain, and after years of hiding, she knew the truth. "It was you." And suddenly, the woman who Cain had thought of as his angel since he was a boy was staring at him with a hatred that could destroy everything.

Keegan smiled brightly as tears streamed down my mother's face. "The irony is just exhilarating! Here we are, with everyone just furious at my supposedly terrible behavior, when we discover that Cain here did something despicable! And to top it off, blamed it on me!" I looked around at our group, people who had stood by us based on Cain's word alone and watched them look at him as if he were a stranger passing by on the street. They may not have known Bo directly, but they knew of him, and they thought of him as a hero, a victim caught up in

Keegan's madness. That remained true, but now the question of whose victim he was had two answers.

Jordyn shouted from the crowd. "Claire, he had to. Bo wouldn't have been able to keep quiet. He would have destroyed everything. Not because he wanted to, but because this bastard would have systematically broke him. He almost broke Cain, and Cain had lots of practice being ripped apart by a man like him. If he could almost get to Cain, he can get to anyone."

"Oh, so you knew too? Did everyone?" She looked around at all the faces staring at her. "That was *not* his decision to make!" she hissed her words, each one dripping with hate. But, Jordyn wasn't the one she was truly angry with, and once she was done with her, she approached Cain, slowly, methodically. "He was a good man. A truly good man who got caught up in something awful simply because he loved me." She swallowed hard and looked toward the ground, and I noticed despite the crowd, not a person spoke a word. The townspeople seemed to understand that something was breaking in front of them, something profound and something terrible. After regaining her composure, she stared straight into Cain's eyes. "How? How did you do it?"

"Claire…"

"Did you surprise him? Or did you put him on his knees like a criminal?"

"Please…"

"Answer me!"

The single act that had defined Cain's destiny more than any other, more than killing his father, more than escaping America, had come back to him, as we had always feared it would. And it made him fall to his knees. "Claire, I can't tell you how sorry I am. It was the worst thing I've ever had to do."

Her voice grew quiet. "Just tell me, Cain. Please. You owe me that much."

As I looked up at Cain and my mother, I tried to make eye contact with him, but to no avail. It seemed like the rest of the world had faded away, and all he could see was her as he began reliving the worst moment of his life. "We sat on the beach for a while, just a while. He looked at the sunset, and as he did, it slowly dawned on him that he was about to die. I pulled out a picture of you, him, and Riley, and even in that moment of sheer, all-encompassing realization of his last minutes on earth, he smiled." I tasted salt on my lips. "Then, I gave him back his cross necklace, the one from his first wife, and he clutched it tightly in his hands." My body shook as I listened. Somehow, even as she listened to the story, my mother found the love within herself to wrap her hands around Cain's. "I stood up, and I willed myself to stop trembling. I didn't want to do it, Claire, I swear it. I stood behind him…he didn't feel anything."

He couldn't look at her, not until he felt her hand on his cheek. With that simple touch, the guilt that he'd been holding in for all those years came flooding out and, like a mother with her child, he collapsed into her arms and she held him against her lap as he sobbed. "I put him down like a dog, Claire…he didn't deserve that."

I barely heard Keegan as he spoke, hovering over them. He feigned concern. "I've never seen you in such a state." He leaned closer. "Pathetic." I watched as he turned to face our group, letting his people hear his every word. "This is your leader? This is the person you want to risk your lives for? I'd think long and hard about whose side you're on, and if you're sure it's the right one. Yes, I've killed people, but you know that. But him? He killed an unarmed man who meant him no harm. Is that really someone you want to align yourself with? To trust? From his own admission, that man's death wasn't self-defense…it was an execution." As he spoke, he nodded at his men, letting them know that it was time to put Cain back on the scaffolding. He fought against them as they tore him from my mother.

"Claire! I'm sorry, I'm so sorry." He was able to slip out one more apology before the rope was around his neck once more.

I could feel the entire crowd waiting, wondering if our group was going to turn right back around from where we came. No sound echoed around us as our group, the townspeople, and even the soldiers waited to see what my mother would do; damn Cain for his deeds or stand by him at the time he needed her the most. Slowly, she walked toward him and did the thing that everyone, even I, least expected. We watched as she stepped up onto the scaffolding next to Cain and, in a gesture that shook us all, slid the extra rope closest to Cain around her own neck. "I forgive you," she said. She faced her audience once again, and they gazed at her with all-encompassing attention. This was her moment, the time that she had yearned for, a chance to fix what she had broken. "If this man deserves to have a rope around his neck, then so do I." I fought the urge to pass out, and Dom had to hold onto me to keep me from running toward them both. "This man has spent his whole life saving people from the Task Force, people who were paid to tear families apart, some of whom you now trust to guard yours. He's the one who spent his childhood, a time that is supposed to be full of love and living dreams, saving other children from being separated from their parents, families representing what he himself never had. Cain spent every second of the past ten years thinking of all of you and doing what needed to be done to protect you." She stared at him, letting him know that the last part of her speech was for him. "…sometimes at the expense of his own soul."

A rumble of dissent started in the crowd. People started toward the scaffolding where Keegan, my mother, and Cain stood. I heard people yelling, remembering what my mother had told them when she first started speaking and finally comparing notes with each other: a husband who met with a mysterious accident, a seventeen-year-old girl who went to the market and never came back. They were starting to realize that living under the veil of it's-their-problem-not-mine when someone disappeared had put their own families at risk, something that I asked myself, now that they had the chance, would they be able to forgive themselves for the part that they had played in Keegan's elaborate charade. When they had time to reflect, would they realize that their own inaction was partially to blame for the demise of the ones they loved? Or, since they had chosen complacency over family, could they claim they really loved them at all?

As they approached, more and more of Keegan's men flooded out to shield him. "Get back!" they shouted. "Get back or we'll shoot you where you stand." Despite the citizens turning against him, Keegan's face was still one of steely resolve. He had not lost yet, and he was searching for a solution to help him keep it that way. He still had protection, and he would use it to his advantage.

In the commotion, I ran over to Ford. "We've won the people over."

He looked at me with a certainty in his eyes. "Yes, but until we win his guards, we've won nothing." My confidence disappeared as quickly as it came. He was right. They were the key to the whole kingdom toppling over.

"Untie me."

I quickly snapped off the zip tie that bound his hands. He looked at me and grabbed my face, gently pulling me to him and kissing me on the forehead as he did the first time I had thought I'd lost him for good. "It's going to be all right. No matter what happens to me, everything is going to be all right." Before I could stop him, he ran toward two bales of hay that were leaned up against one of the tall street lanterns that sprinkled the square. He shouted over the crowd. "Please! Guards! Listen to me. I'm one of you. If you've ever believed me before, believe me now. I've stood beside you in defense of our home. I've pulled you to safety when we thought there was none. This man is not who he says he is."

As Ford spoke, Keegan's visage started to crack. The face that always appeared so confident and sure started to contort, the expression of one trying to keep his rage a secret started to show itself. "Shut up."

"He isn't General Cole, he's Marcus Keegan. He was the head of the Task Force, the people that ripped your children from your arms and laughed as you helplessly watched. He's the one responsible for taking your children away from you in the first place!"

"I told you to shut up. You just spill lies." He faced the guards, his veneer melting away and revealing the devil in its place. "Don't believe him. He's been poisoned by the man standing in front of you. Don't listen to a word."

But they *were* listening. As Ford spoke, more and more of Keegan's soldiers lowered their weapons. And as Keegan removed the revolver from his holster, he would do the one thing that would seal his fate forever. The shot rang out, and as Ford fell to the ground, a deafening silence filled the air, one that I wasn't sure would ever go away.

CHAPTER EIGHTEEN

Riley

"No!" I ran to Ford's side and knelt beside him, blood pouring out of him like oil from the soft earth. "Don't leave us…don't leave me, please. I'm sorry."

Ford winced with every word. "I'm the one who's sorry."

"Please, Ford, hang on. This is all my fault." Even as I said the words, I had seen enough gunshot wounds to know that we were spending the last precious seconds together that we would ever have.

"No, no, please, Riley…this was the plan all along. We knew it would be one of us. I'm glad it was me." I wanted to ask what he meant, but he started to cough, and I knew our time was growing short.

We grasped each other's hands. "You have been one of the most precious things in my life. Please, know that." He coughed again, then said, "Tell me a story. Something true."

Shattered Night

My breath hitched inside me. "Remember that time where we stole some extra cheese from the compound refrigerator to feed that stray cat we found?"

His voice cracked. "Ugly thing it was. But it made you so happy."

I had so many stories, so many memories. But as his blood covered my hands, I struggled to think of only one. "...and the time that I had a nightmare and knocked on your window in the dead of night to go on a walk with me?"

"We walked for hours," he said. The color was draining from his cheeks, like water out of a bath, slowly leaving him with nothing.

"You were there, always there. I'll never forget that. I swear it."

Though he was weakening before me, he smiled. "This...all of this...it was all worth it."

"Why?" I sobbed.

"It was worth it to see the way you are looking at me right now." I felt the grip he had on my hand loosen, and I lay it on his chest. I stared at him for a moment, hardly able to comprehend that I was going to have to say goodbye to yet another friend, another good person who got caught in the middle of the mess that was Cain's and my life, all because he had the nerve to care for me, despite every reason I had given him not to.

I looked around at Ford's fellow guards. They had all seen what Keegan had done, and they stared at him with scathing eyes. "You shot him down like a dog in the street. He was one of us, and you pulled that trigger like he was nothing."

"Ford was good to us," another said.

"I believe him." Voices of support rang out. Some of the guards turned their faces away, trying to hide the display of emotion they were having for their fallen friend, someone who they had started to listen to, but all too late.

"I believe him too." Slowly, almost every guard that had been protecting Keegan distanced themselves from him, filtering into the crowd, and in the process, becoming part of the townspeople. The division between the ruling body and the ruled disintegrated, and they all became one unit again, a collective that was ready for the change we were hoping for.

A handful of guards stayed at Keegan's side, but from the glare in his eye that pierced the people around him, I could tell he knew that he had lost. "You're all useless. I made you something important. Now, you're nothing. Nothing!" He fired a shot right above the crowd. "Come on!" He and his men ran as fast as they could toward the house, but on his way, he took the time to kick the board out from Cain's feet, and I watched as the man I loved was lifted into the air by his throat.

Dominic and I raced up to the scaffolding as Cain started to turn blue. While my attention had been on Ford, my mother had removed the rope from her neck, and she was now trying to hold Cain up until we could get there. Though she gripped him with every ounce of strength she had, it wasn't working. His skin was turning red against the rope, and his body unconsciously kicked trying to free itself, the same as our friends' had weeks before.

Shattered Night

"Hang on!" we shouted, pushing people out of our way with the force that came when life and death are separated by split seconds. By the time we got through the crowd and cut the rope down, Cain's breath was barely audible.

He fell against me and reached up to rub his throat, as I finally got to say the words that I had feared I would never get to say again. "I love you, Cain, I love you more than you will ever know."

Dom, my mother, and I held him close, and after a couple minutes, he embraced us in return. "I love you. All of you."

I sat there in his arms for a few cherished moments. I had thought I was going to lose him for the last time as I saw him there, his feet kicking toward life, yet we had somehow found our way back to each other. But until that very second, I was sure that was not going to be the case. "Cain, before he died, Ford told me that he 'knew it was going to be one of us.' What was he talking about?" An inkling of something started to form in the back of my mind, but I needed Cain to give it life.

Cain hesitated. "We had to make sure that Keegan lost power. Ford figured out a way to do that and keep the rest of the people we love safe."

"You left us. You had promised you wouldn't do that to me again. You took my choice away."

"I know, Riley. I'm sorry. But I knew you would have never let me go, and potentially sacrifice myself otherwise. And I had hoped if I left right before the battle you and the rest of our group would hate me enough not to come after me."

The pieces started to form in my head. I slapped

him across the face. "How could you ever think anything you did would make me love you any less? After everything we've been through. You could have done anything, and I would still have been right beside you. You leaving doesn't make me as angry as you believing that you could do anything to dissuade me from loving you. If Ford hadn't shown up, we would have been right outside that gate."

He brushed my cheek. "Poor, cursed beauty. Look at the perfect mess we are."

Kissing his forehead, I said, "But we're our own. And that's what matters. Now please, tell me what happened."

"I spoke to Ford right before I turned myself in. I asked him to take care of you in my place. Of course, he berated me for turning myself in, knowing I would be breaking your heart. But when I explained to him why, that I knew we were going into a battle we couldn't win, we decided to work together so we could ensure the survival of not only our people, but the country itself. So we came up with a plan."

"But you still turned yourself in."

"We knew one of two things would happen. Either Keegan would kill me, and Ford would have to help you continue the fight without me, or Keegan would send people to get the rest of you to bring you all in. If he killed me, Ford would still be here to warn you and get you all to safety. I hoped that you would hate me enough for leaving you that you would leave this place without question. After he made sure you were all gone, he would have

Shattered Night

come back and set the helicopters on fire. We wanted to do that as a last resort because if we didn't kill Keegan's image, he would be able to regroup with all his followers and pick up right where he left off, but at least that would have bought him some time. But if Keegan decided to bring you all in to make sure he could keep me under his control…well, that's when Ford would be ready."

It started to make sense. "So there'd be less of them. Their numbers would be smaller, and we would have a chance."

"I didn't want anyone else I loved to die for me." He stared at me. "I'm tired, Riley. I'm tired of people dying, and I'm tired of fighting. This was supposed to be one more fight, no matter how it went." I grabbed his hand, and all the memories we shared passed between us like electricity. "We still had to kill the love the people and his guards had for him." He embraced me. "We hoped that Claire could turn everyone, and she did an amazing job with the townspeople. I knew there was a chance you couldn't make it in time to save me from the inevitable rope around my neck, though it would have been worth it. But my death would not be enough to sway the guards if Claire was unable to. We knew if we had to, the guards would understand the man they were truly following if they saw Keegan shoot one of their own. He had built his army on principles of family and loyalty, and if he ruined that, he would ruin everything."

My stomach turned and I fought the urge to vomit. I whispered as the realization sunk in. "Ford provoked him on purpose." My mouth went dry. "He died to save us all."

"He was a brave man. He wanted to make it right. All of it."

Suddenly, Jordyn's voice loomed over us. "Then let's make sure he did."

We followed her to the front of the crowd that had gathered just outside Keegan's house. "They're inside. Keegan and the rest of his guys. A few stayed with him. Hardcore loyalists, I guess," Nick said.

"Loyalty isn't going to save them this time. They've never met an enemy that they didn't hear coming. Until today," I said.

Reagan came up to Cain and me, his expression hardened with grief. "Well, Cain, it looks like you're going to get your battle after all." He was silent as he walked back to the place where Ford had fallen. I watched as he knelt beside him, and my heart broke in two as I saw his body shake from the sobs that we all knew would come.

As Cain, Jordyn, Nick, and I turned to the door, I knew that he was right.

The rest of our group looked at us. Though they all wanted to join, we knew we couldn't leave the townspeople or all of Keegan's men unattended. They had only just decided to be one of us, and we couldn't afford to risk anyone changing their minds. "Go," Olivia said as she grasped my hands. "Go, but come back."

I hugged her tightly. "Take care of Reagan. We will be all right."

As the rest of us faced the house, Cain cried out,

"I'm not going to give you some long speech, something about why we need to do this and what we stand for. We do this for Ford, and for everyone we've lost." Our people cheered, knowing victory was almost upon us. Dom briefly came up to us, and with no words exchanged between us, nodded and gave us his blessing. His expression was that of a father sending his child off to war, something we had unfortunately seen countless times before that day.

Cain turned to face the house along with the three of us but cried out so all could hear, "We're coming for you, you sonofabitch...we're coming for you."

But the second we started toward the door, we realized the fight we yearned for may still not come to pass. Because just as we took our first steps, Keegan emerged yet again, this time, with a gun aimed at Xander and McKenzie's heads.

CHAPTER NINETEEN

Riley

"I would stay back if I were you," Keegan yelled loud enough so the whole crowd could hear, the few loyal guards he still had flanking him on either side with guns in hand. "The good news is, I may only be able to kill one before you kill me. But which one will it be?" He maneuvered his gun between his two potential victims.

Jordyn started to race toward him, but Cain held her back. "You sonofabitch! Let them go! I'll kill you. I swear!"

We all stood at the ready, our hands hovering over our weapons. But at that moment, we knew we couldn't attack. Keegan had the upper hand, and this time, if we made the wrong decision, two children would die, the last members of Jordyn's family that she had left. "I'm going to be heading in now. If you would like to see your precious kin again, I'd advise you not to follow me."

As he slammed the door and locked it behind

him, a group of guards came up to us. "We can help you get in. We know this place inside and out."

Cain shook his head. "No, it's too risky."

"We need to get them out!" Jordyn cried.

"I know, but if he hears us coming, that will be the end of those kids. We can't risk it."

"Well, what the hell do you propose we do then?"

Maynard smiled, then reminded us of one very important element. "I checked. With all the commotion, they never got the power back on to this building. Other than the life-support systems, they're running dark."

The group of us made our way back to Adam's tent, where we opened the drawings that my mother had helped us steal. When we found the one of Keegan's house, we sat it in the middle of Adam's potting bench so that everyone could see it. "Our first priority is to free the hostages," Cain said as he pointed to a spot on the drawing. "According to this drawing, Keegan has a small jail cell in the basement of that house." He turned to Adam. "If I had to guess, this is where he kept the people who were thought to have disappeared until he killed them. No one but the sick and people who he specifically invited ever entered that place, so they would not be seen."

"I would have to assume that place will be heavily guarded. He has to know we're coming for them."

"Yes, which is why you will be the ones freeing them. He's going to expect me and Jordyn the most, so we are going to head to him first. With any luck, he will suspect that we came to kill him before freeing the hostages."

Just then, a guard emerged at the end of Adam's tent. "Adam, there are some people here that wanted to see you." As he spoke, seven new faces emerged from behind him. Without a word, Adam ran toward them. "Thank God you are all ok!"

"The guard let us out and told us what happened. You did it, Adam!" A woman from the new group said.

He turned to me. "No, she did." Then pointing to all of us, he said, "All of these people did. They risked their lives to save us all."

The woman who had spoken came up to me and wrapped her hands around mine. "You are an angel. All of you are."

"I'm just glad you are all ok." She released my hands as her and the rest of Adam's friends left. "Are you going to follow them? I'm sure you have a lot to catch up on."

Adam shook his head. "You saved us. I'm not going to forget that. I'm going to help you get those children, or die in the attempt."

Without a word, I nodded, and we went back to the drawing, deciding how exactly we would get them out without Adam or any of us having to follow through on that commitment.

We waited till the cover of night, at the edge of the village, and marched toward the house where they were being held, fanning out as we approached so as not to be seen. We would be the silent soldiers we had been trained to be.

As a unit, we swarmed the house, crawling

through any crevice, hiding around every corner, waiting for just the right time to dispatch anyone in our way. To my right, I saw Verita run her knife through a guard as he raised a bullhorn to his lips, quieting his alarm. After hearing a noise behind me, I turned around to see Nyla slice open the neck of a man who had been coming toward me with his own blade raised. I looked at her with a quiet thank you as we made our way toward the center of the house.

This was the battle we were meant to fight. Under the cover of darkness, their guns didn't matter. Without the luxury of sight, guns were no match for our silence.

I looked over to see Cain, the man I loved, sending another person to his death. How did love and death become so intertwined for us? It wasn't supposed to be that way. Love was supposed to exist by itself, pure and true, without blood raining down upon it. As I felt my own blade plunge into the flesh of another, I wondered if we'd ever find a way to have one exist without the other.

We moved as one, in the same way we had when we fought together the first time. But this time, our one was not two, but several, and all people that we would give our lives to protect. As we moved together, we knew they would do the same for us, as we all shielded each other from any oncoming storm. And as the last man in sight fell, I knew we had succeeded.

Our group gathered, taking a mental count of who was with us. When I saw someone missing, my stomach dropped. "Where's Nick?"

Dom looked at me with panic in his eyes. "I

don't know."

Our answer came quickly as a guard revealed himself with a knife to Nick's throat. "I'm leaving this place. You will let me leave this place, or so help me, he dies."

Dom slowly inched closer to him. "Put the knife down and we will let you walk out of here. You have my word."

"This is what your word means to me!" The guard said as he sliced a shallow cut into Nick's shoulder. "The next one will kill him, I mean it!" He started dragging Nick toward the door. I looked at Dom and he looked at me, and I knew in my gut that we both understood how this would end if we didn't act. Without a moment's hesitation, Dom reached for a chair that was sitting in the hall and charged at the guard. In the attempt to shield himself, he dropped the knife as the chair came down on top of his head. Nick fell to the ground and I pulled him away from the struggle as quickly as I could. Another guard came out of the closet where, apparently, he'd been hiding, and attempted to aid his friend, only to have Dom effortlessly flip the chair around in his grasp and hit him with it full force.

When he was finished, both men lay still.

Cain came up to him and put a hand on Dom's shoulder. In response, he said, "I guess you did need the convict." He looked toward the floor, where both bodies seemed to call for his attention. I hoped there would be a day where he could forget their faces, and not think about what he'd done that day, but I knew that wouldn't be possible. Not for him.

Shattered Night

"We will need the priest again. When this is done, it will be time for you to take charge of this place."

Dom stepped back. "What about you?"

"I am the fighter, Dom. You're the leader. It's your time to lead." There was a look exchanged between them, silent memories that passed through the air that I would never know, or completely understand. "I'm going to help get those children."

Dom turned to head to the jail when Adam raced toward us. "They aren't there. The kids aren't in there. It's completely empty."

The realization settled in my stomach like a brick. "They're with him. He's got them with him."

Jordyn looked at me, and said, "Then let's hunt him down."

It stood to reason that Keegan would barricade himself in the storage room so he could hide out for as long as possible. With so few men who remained loyal to him, he couldn't afford to make a mistake. He had to hide and figure a way out of his impossible situation.

But he didn't. Instead, we found the large dining room door locked shut. "This is an easy lock. Give me ten seconds, and I can pick it." Nick started on it, and as he predicted, it unlocked in a matter of seconds. As he examined it, we sent everyone outside except for me, Cain, Nick, and Jordyn. Though in theory, it would seem good to keep the numbers, we knew if too many came at him at once, we risked him mowing us all down in gunfire, including the children.

As I watched Nick with the lock, uneasiness

swept over me, and I grabbed Cain's shoulder. "Wait a minute. This is too easy. Something doesn't feel right."

"She's right, Cain. Stay here with Riley and let me do it. I need to. Please," Jordyn said, desperation dripping from her voice so much that the sound made my gut scream even louder. Every ounce of me knew that this was not what it appeared to be. Something was wrong.

Cain put his hand on Jordyn's shoulder. "You're my sister. I'd do anything for you. I'd give you my life. But I won't give you this." He kissed her cheek. "You have been by my side through all of this. I am the man I am today," he smiled at me, "and am able to love a woman like her because of you." He turned to Nick. "I'm so very proud of you, more than you will ever know. You are every ounce the man I hoped you would be, and more. Thank you for your kindness, and your vast, forgiving heart. It's more than I deserve." Nick and Jordyn looked at each other as he turned to me. "I love you more than the world itself." I stared at him, his words to all of us echoing in my head, and knew that there was something in them that was permanent, unchanging.

He was saying goodbye.

He faced Jordyn one more time. "We do this together." And with that, he shoved me and Nick away and disappeared through the door with Jordyn, sealing it shut behind him.

CHAPTER TWENTY

Keegan

There was no question that Cain would come for me. In a way, I couldn't blame him. We had played a game, and he had won. At least, it appeared that way.

I sat down in a chair in the dining room area. I had people gathering Xander and McKenzie for me, and it was very possible that those precious minutes alone were going to be my last on earth. I'd always valued quiet, but as a people fought for their lives very close by in the house, I knew that was one thing that would be lost to me forever. People were living and dying mere feet from where I was and all I wanted to do was sit in silence just one more time.

One more thing that Cain had taken from me.

People always tell you to think of happy memories right before you're about to die. But as I searched my mind, I realized mine were very few and far between. Perhaps that was my price to pay for my sins, of which there were far too many.

The moment I found most easily was of myself, about seven or eight, sitting on a swing in the park, back when the city was keeping them clean and safe. I saw sand below me, and crisp green grass beyond that. There was a rocking horse to my right, the playground kind that sat on a spring. To my left sat a slide, with a tall, red ladder that at the time seemed monstrous. I'd never been brave enough to climb it, but the swing was enough for me.

I sat on that swing for as long as my mother would allow it. Where I was a coward when it came to the ladder, I was a warrior when it came to that swing. Higher and higher I would go, until I imagined I was toying on the edge of flipping over the steel bar that it hung from, into a victorious giant summersault before I came back toward the earth again.

The last time I was there, the sky was the same blue as my brand-new sneakers. I remember that. Of all the stupid, inconsequential things to remember in the last moments of one's life, I remembered that. They stretched out in front of me as I swung, and as I drifted higher and higher, I looked down below me at the other kids. I was braver than them, taller, faster. And for that moment, I was *better*. I supposed I had spent most of my life still on that swing, chasing the power that I felt soaring above those destined to shuffle about at my feet.

I longed to take one last look at what I'd built, but I was trapped. So I had to settle for picturing the village, *my village*, in my mind alone. I had rebuilt a country, or at least a part of it. People had civilization again…purpose. And that was what I would leave behind.

I looked down at the object sitting at my feet and smiled. I had chosen the way I would die. It would be painful, yes, but fitting. No ordinary death would do, not for me. I needed an exit as large, as vast as my accomplishments. I needed a death that would be remembered. As I grasped the object in my hand, I knew it would.

CHAPTER TWENTY-ONE

Cain

I heard Riley screaming from behind the door, pounding her fists against it. "Cain! Don't do this! Please!" As Jordyn covered me, I shoved a nearby piece of furniture against the door for extra strength.

Riley was not going to die today.

Keegan smiled. "It sounds like someone is calling for you. Maybe you better go to her." Xander and McKenzie sat in chairs near Keegan, feet and hands bound. I noticed he had a gas lantern in his hands, and his plan took shape. If he was going to die, he wanted to take me with him.

"This is between us." Jordyn stood at my side, as it had always been, but instead of a gun in her hand, she held a knife. Her focus was true and steady, and I saw a fire within her that I hadn't seen since Micah had died, and it broke me in two knowing that it came from the fact that she was about to kill again.

"I beg to differ. You made it between all of us

Shattered Night

when you brought all your people here." He paused and then gestured around the room. "Fitting that our story should end like this, isn't it? With fire raging around us, a fire that was started by me this time?" As he said this, he tossed the lantern into the air and it shattered onto the ground. He had thrown it next to the curtains, and within moments they were engulfed in flames.

The smoke billowed around us, thick and heavy. Several of Keegan's guards were still there, refusing to leave their leader behind to save themselves. Admirable, I had to admit. If they survived what was about to happen, they would be valuable assets for Father Dominic.

But that was not to be. Because as they each came at me, our suspicions were confirmed. Though they may have had weapons, using them was not second-nature. As soon as they raised their guns, we knocked them from their grip, and they clanged against the floor as they fell. Quickly, and almost regretfully, Jordyn and I dispatched each of them, and their bodies crashed down, leaving a trail of flesh to Keegan's feet.

I didn't want to. Their intentions were good; they were just aimed in the wrong direction. With no guard to shield him, Jordyn and I approached him and shoved him toward the ground. Quickly, Jordyn ran to her brother and stepdaughter's sides, untying them with the speed of someone who had been escaping places her whole life. "I need you to get out of here. There's a window up there." She pointed to a window hovering above us, only accessible by standing on a buffet server under it and jumping to grab the ledge. "When you get out, go straight to a woman named Olivia. She will protect you." After a bit of protest, Xander helped McKenzie up and out, then climbed out himself.

Keegan kneeled in front of us, and I relieved him of his sidearm. "Such a shame. Those were good men that you just murdered. But you don't call it murder, do you? You always find a way to justify yourself, yet you look at me with disgust. There's more than one killer in this room, Cain. Don't you forget that."

As I plunged my knife toward his throat for the second and last time, I assured him I never would.

But, as if it had separated itself from me completely, my hand stopped just at the edge of his skin.

I had been there before, in the position to execute an unarmed man. I felt my hand start to tremble. Bo's face appeared in my mind's eye, with the sad smile it'd had when he felt in his soul that I was about to take his life from him, a life that he had deserved to keep. Keegan did not deserve my mercy, but dispatching a man who had no means to save himself for a second time made my guts turn inside out. The last time I had done it, it had nearly ruined me, and it took Riley to bring me back. I didn't know if I could recover from it again. A maniacal laughter came from below me. "What's a matter? You can't do it? Cain Foley, the bringer of death and destruction, the man who kills anyone who he deems unworthy, can't do it." He continued to face out. "What about if I tell you about those girls? How they looked when their bodies fell, helpless to save themselves. Or what if I tell you about what I plan to do to your lovely Claire if I get out of here? I'm going to put that rope back around her neck and squeeze it tight myself. Then I might loosen it, just a little, just to give her a split second of hope so that I can snuff it out again." Every muscle in my body shook, and I put more pressure on the blade, but I still couldn't press through. I looked at the knife in my hand, and I looked at Keegan. Instantly, I realized, the thing I wanted most of all, was not his death, but to feel the life in my soul once again. But as the flames closed in, I was sure I never would.

CHAPTER TWENTY-TWO

Riley

Dominic had to physically carry me out of Keegan's house. I didn't know where he had come from, but as I clung to the door, which was getting hotter by the second, I knew he was the only one strong enough to tear me away. From what sounded like some distant place, I heard him say, "We can't go in now…even if we get the door open…it's too late…"

When the battle was over, we all gathered in the center of town to regroup. The soldiers who had served Keegan were lined up in a row, all sitting on the ground with their hands tied in their laps, allowing us to have that extra second we may need if anyone suddenly decided to become a Keegan sympathizer once again. I heard Verita reassure them that it was just a precaution and that they would be free shortly. I searched the faces of my comrades for the one that I needed to see most of all. "Where is he?"

Shattered Night

Everyone looked at each other, hoping that someone else would know something they didn't. Olivia met me near the center of the square with Xander and McKenzie trailing behind her and asked a question that sent a bolt of electricity throughout my body. "I don't see Cain. Where did he go?"

"He's not out here yet?" I asked, already knowing the answer.

"No, I haven't seen him. No one has...Jordyn either..." Her voice trailed off. Without a word, I ran toward the house.

When we got to the room where Cain had locked me out, I still couldn't get in. "Here, let me try." I turned around to see Dominic, Reagan, and Nick standing behind me. They picked up a large beam that was lying in the debris that used to be part of Keegan's house. Between the three of them, they were able to break the door down.

The fire that had started behind the closed doors had spread throughout the room. I saw an open window, but neither Cain nor Jordyn had been outside, and the realization that he was still in the room made my limbs grow numb.

Keegan's body was barely identifiable. The burnt flesh on his face had become a flaky collection of beige and red. The clothes he'd had on had stuck to his skin and I couldn't tell one kind of fabric from another. The only thing I recognized was the metal belt he was wearing, the one that had the symbol of the deer eating a snake that I remembered from the first day we arrived. I had a brief moment of relief when I realized none of the bodies were female, meaning however she had managed it, Jordyn was safe.

The only thing I recognized on the body next to Keegan was a wedding ring. I recognized it because I had slipped it on his finger just a short time ago. Dominic and Reagan lunged toward me and as the world turned white, I prayed I would never wake up again.

My wish was not granted. When I regained consciousness after what could have been hours or days, I found myself on top of a bed. Olivia and my mother were both there, along with Nick. I wondered where Jordyn had gone but at the moment I didn't care. I looked at Olivia. "See, I told you we would be ok." It was only then that I remembered what I had seen, and my breath came and went in huge gulps. When I saw Dominic praying in the corner by my bed, I knew it was over. "Tell me it isn't true." They were silent. "Mom?"

She didn't need to say it, I could see it on her face, but she said it anyway, "I can't."

Cain had a soldier's funeral, the kind he deserved. Everyone from town showed up. If someone had just arrived, they would have seen an empty city, with shut-down stores, no trace smiling at each other as they passed by, just a vast nothingness. It would have looked much like the rest of the old America, right before the collapse. How everything had changed, but everything had still remained the same. The thought comforted me and made me sick simultaneously.

Jordyn never returned. Before she had left, she told Xander and McKenzie that Olivia would look after them. Olivia didn't sign up to be a new

Shattered Night

mother, but she kept the promise made on her behalf. Though I missed Jordyn, I understood. She had known Cain longer than almost anyone, and if she had to deal with losing him by running away from the memories, so be it.

I had been too distraught to go to Ford's memorial service, but everyone told me he was given the respect he had earned. His fellow guards came and saluted him, folding an American flag into a triangle and laying it at his side. Reagan was inconsolable, but I was glad to know that Olivia had remained by his side, holding his hand as he grieved for the friend he had chosen to be his brother.

The guilt that I had, knowing Ford died partially to earn my forgiveness weighed upon me heavily, and every time I heard a loud noise, his death happened to me all over again. But even that deep, endless guilt was nothing compared to the grief I felt when I realized that Cain was gone forever. He was not off on some mission, saving the country's children from their suffering, he was lying there, quiet and lost to the world, one that would be an entirely different place without him in it.

We laid Cain's body gently on a wooden slab, wrapped in a white sheet. Adam and Reagan were kind enough to take care of his body so that Dominic and I didn't have to. Seeing what was left of him the first time was too much, and seeing him again would have made me shut down altogether. After he was placed there, Olivia, my mother, and I surrounded him with bright yellow flowers that we'd found growing scattered around the village, and some of the townspeople brought flowers from their own gardens. A trace of smoke still billowed from the rubble that had been Keegan's house, reminding me as it snaked into the air that Keegan was gone, but it had come with a price that if I had a chance to do it over, I would not have paid. I didn't care about the rest of the world, not anymore. Because if I could have sacrificed the country to have just one more minute with Cain, I would have done so gladly.

I would have set it on fire and smiled as I let the match fall through the air.

I started to take my place next to Nick so I could help carry him when I felt a tap on my shoulder. Two of the originals that Cain had rescued were standing there. The girl said, "You've carried him enough. Please, let us do this. For both him and for you." I glanced behind me to see my mother, face swollen, but waiting with open arms for me to run to her as I did when I was a child, waiting for me to do the only thing I could think of that might help me get through the next few minutes. As I looked at their faces, I remembered that I was not the only one who was grieving, and maybe they needed to do one last act for Cain as much as I needed to pretend it wasn't real.

"Thank you," I said as I stepped aside. As I fell into my mother's arms, I thought about how we had come back to each other. And at that very moment, I was so glad that we had, because if I hadn't had her there, I would have fallen right to the ground.

The only one that dared talk to me before the service was Adam. "Thank you," he said softly. "Thank you for all that you have done."

Shattered Night

I stared at him hard. "Make this place better. Because I will tell you right now," I gestured toward the white sheet, "nothing was worth this. Nothing."

He paused, probably trying to come up with a response that would ease my pain, but quickly figured out that nothing could. With a small nod, he walked back into the crowd, and the warm embrace of his friends whom would have died without us.

Dominic made a wonderful speech, probably filled with beautiful memories of the past, and some words that were supposed to have made me feel like there was some sort of hope for the future. And perhaps for some, his words helped them heal, if only a little. The fact that he could stand there, mighty and tall, without crumbling into a million pieces as I was doing was a testament to his faith because I knew the fact that he was somehow keeping himself together didn't mean he was any less devastated. He was in Cain's life even before I was, and I knew he wouldn't know how to go on without him any more than I did.

But I didn't hear any of his beautiful speech. As he lit the final match that would send Cain to the God that he, Bo, and Dom all loved with every bit of themselves, I vomited toward the ground and turned away.

The next morning, as I tried to hold on to one more minute of restless sleep, I knew I was not alone. All I could see was the wall, but I could sense her presence as she entered my room. She didn't have to say a word, but she did. "How are you?"

"Mom, do you think everything's tainted now?"

"What do you mean?" She sat down on my bed.

"I mean, can there ever really be any happy times after you lose someone you love? Like even if something good happens, is it still sad because the first thing you think of is 'oh I would love for him to be here for this, and he can't?' Is anything ever right again? Because right now, it doesn't feel like I can breathe, let alone live my life."

"Turn around." It took all my strength, but I did, my body heavy and almost unyielding. "When your father left, I didn't think I'd ever enjoy anything again. He didn't die, but he left of his own free will. It's not the same kind of pain that you're going through, it's different, but it's still pain, the kind that sticks on you like a second skin." She tucked a strand of hair behind my ear, but this time, the motherly gesture did nothing. "For a while, you just go through the motions. Every minute, every second takes work. And that's ok. You go through the motions because it's all you can do. And every day, it gets just a little bit easier."

"Does it ever stop hurting?"

My mother paused, like she was considering lying to me, but thought the better of it. "No, it doesn't. There's always going to be something that you wish Cain wasn't missing. But you will learn to find the joy in life again. It won't be easy, but human beings are capable of surviving the worst things in the world, and the worst of all is losing love." She bent down and kissed my forehead. "If I could take this pain from you, I would gladly. I would ball it up and swallow it inside myself so I

Shattered Night

could take it with me wherever I go so you wouldn't have to…but I can't. This is one you are going to have to carry on your own. You've had to carry so many things on your own, and this will be the heaviest. But if one person can do it, it's you. Remember, Riley, to always seek joy, even in the darkest of times. I promise you, if you seek it out, even in the smallest moments, you will find it."

As she left, there was no doubt in my mind that she was wrong.

***

One year later, the village had gotten somewhat back to normal. We all had our own living quarters, and Dominic and my mother ran things together. It seemed fitting, and I thought Cain would have wanted it that way. My mother had a chance to continue what she'd done in the square, and put a little piece of the country that she'd destroyed back together. Dominic had traded a congregation for a whole village. And of course, he had the most generous heart out of all of us. When he suggested ways for all of us to live together in peace, his enthusiasm was contagious, and the other villagers, even the ones who may have missed the Keegan days, couldn't help but love him. I don't think you have to love a leader for him to lead, but it sure helps when you do. I even noticed some of that love starting to soften my mother's heart, as I caught them holding hands on more than one occasion. After Bo, it hadn't appeared she would give herself a chance to be loved again. But, perhaps helping bring down Keegan had given her the sense of penance that none of us could have provided her on our own. As I gazed at them, talking quietly and laughing with one another, I felt elated and sick all at once, realizing that I would never look at anyone the way they looked at each other, ever again.

People were permitted to have weapons again, but they chose not to use them, this time, of their own volition, not someone else's. Some homes had several, and some had none, and all were permitted to protect their families as they saw fit. And if for some reason someone tried to take from us what we had made of a false society, all of us would be able to defend it. Together.

I'm not proud of how I acted as we all tried to start over. When Olivia and Nick weren't practically carrying me home from the bar, they were blessedly letting themselves be on the receiving end of my screaming. I'd smashed practically everything in our living quarters, and at one point I'm told I had punched Verita in the face for telling me I looked awful and I needed to go talk to someone (she was right on both counts).

The only salvation I had was trying to put the town back together. Physically, it was never broken, but since the fire, they desperately needed a new hospital (a regretful outcome of Keegan's last stand) and I needed something to throw myself into that wasn't a ravine.

The moments of peace that I did have involved smashing hammers into nails, and sawing boards so they would fit where they needed to go. As the hammer came down, I would relish in the impact,

Shattered Night

and get lost in the consistent, steady sound.

I didn't talk much when I built. The girls tried to get me to, but I ignored them. Dom was the only one who seemed to understand, bringing me water and food and sitting it next to me without making me say a word. Every once in a while, he would wink at me, and I would wink back, some sort of acknowledgment of our shared suffering, and our shared guilt. Was there something I could have done differently that would have saved him? What if we had just left? Why hadn't we just gone away when we had the chance? Maybe he could have been saved if we both hadn't been so obsessed with controlling the outcome of things that maybe we had no business with, in the first place. Perhaps he was asking himself similar questions: what if he hadn't been arrested all those years ago? Maybe Cain never would have started the Guide network, and they would both be back there now…safe and alive, teaching and helping children, just in a different way. I could picture it: Dom giving a sermon as Cain passed out snacks and listened as the parishioners told him stories that he may not have wanted to listen to, but would have just the same, so he could make sure they felt wanted and appreciated in a way they may not experience outside those four walls. Maybe that should have been what was the most important: not the rest of the world, but love. Just plain, ordinary, extraordinary love.

I went to bed after a long day of building, and I almost didn't notice it. I had turned away from it and whipped my head around to make sure that I'd seen what I thought I had.

Cain's little toy soldier, the one he always carried in his pocket every minute of every day, was sitting on my nightstand, perfect and unsinged by flames.

Which meant something much more significant.

"I thought you might want this back." Olivia appeared at the front of our tent. She came over and placed Cain's wedding ring in my hand. I stared at it a moment, putting the pieces together, terrified to believe it, yet terrified not to.

"What? You knew? How could you…you've seen me cry every day for an entire year." Rage and disbelief bubbled within me as I looked into the face of my oldest friend.

She reached for my hands. "It had to be real. Riley, I'm so sorry, but it had to be real. He knew no one would buy it unless you showed real emotion."

I pulled away. "Why? Why would you do this to me? Why would he?"

"He didn't want to. Believe me, the last thing either of us wanted to do was to put you through hell. But he had to. He knew that once Keegan was dead, the bounties on his head would all return. He didn't want that for you, always wondering what was around every corner. So he gave me that, and told me when the time was right, to let you see it, and give you back the ring." She paused. "There was another part to it too. When he left the first time, you knew there was a chance he was still alive. This plan gave you an opportunity to truly see what life could be like without him in it." As she

Shattered Night

took my hands in hers, she continued. "He wanted you to have a choice, to truly give you the chance to decide how you wanted your life to be, without any interference from him. He wanted to give you the chance to move on, to find happiness without him in your life, and maybe meet someone who wouldn't be constantly haunted by his own history. He gave me the task of judging whether or not you could." A slight smile spread across her face. "But you're a mess without him. Clearly. Look at you…it's obvious you aren't going to move on, and never could. No matter how much he might have wanted it for you, the puddle of nothingness that you've turned into proves that was never going to happen."

Even before she'd finished her sentence, I had started to pack a bag. "Will you be all right?"

She smiled. "Of course I will. You gave me something to hold on to, whether you knew it or not."

"What is that?"

She glanced out the open door and I followed her gaze. Standing talking with Nick was Reagan, with a smile across his face like nothing I'd seen since he lost Ford. "You somehow managed to convince me that I could have something special too– maybe not with blatant words, but in sticking by me, and believing in me always. Since you believed, so did I. And now I have him to come home to." My eyes welled with tears, relieved that, after feeling like everyone who dared to care about me ended up hurt or dead, there was someone who I had helped find their way back to themselves. She embraced me. "He said you'd know where to find him."

And I did.

I didn't say goodbye to anyone when I left. I couldn't. If word got out that Cain was still alive, all my suffering, all *his* suffering, it would all be for nothing. But I did leave a little something for Dom under his pillow. I pictured him seeing the soldier looking up at him, and hoped that from seeing that and knowing Cain was still here, even if he was still lost, he would find some peace. I hoped my mother would forgive me, and I tried to tell myself that Dom would make sure she didn't hate me forever. My head said she wouldn't, but my heart said something else.

But in the end, none of it mattered. Because as I boarded the ship to a strange land where I had never been, I knew I was going home.

It took me two weeks to get there, one by cargo ship, the second by bus. The Irish countryside had all become one stream of green. But when I closed the thin log fence behind me, I knew I was exactly where I wanted to be.

There was a gentle wind making the grass sway back and forth when I saw him. He was chopping wood outside a small cabin at the top of a hill, just like what I had pictured when he had told me about his grandparents' property so long ago. There was plenty of wood in a pile next to the side of the house, but he swung the glinting metal into the sky over and over again anyway. I saw smoke billowing from the chimney, and the smell of roasting meat hit me like a cement wall. "I don't think we're going to need all of that." I smiled at him.

"You're probably right."

Shattered Night

We just looked at each other for a moment, frozen in the space that had been between us, afraid to believe that it was over: the running, the hiding, the fighting. But when he wrapped his arms around me, I knew it was true. I took the ring out of my pocket. "Thought you might want this back." He happily stuck his hand out for me to put the ring back on his finger, as I had done when he had asked me to be his wife. As I held his hand, we went inside, and the Irish breeze welcomed us home.

CHAPTER TWENTY-THREE

One Year Earlier

Cain looked at Jordyn, and with resolve in his eyes, he said four words that would change their lives forever. "I can't do it."

"What the hell do you mean?" She attempted to snatch the knife from Cain's shaking hand, but he pulled it away. "Give that to me and I'll do it myself."

He turned to her with an expression that she had seen many times before, one that told her that he would tell her everything later, but for now, she would just have to trust him. "As soon as he dies, the bounties on my head will return full force." He turned to Keegan. "We need his help."

"Oh, Cain, how everything has a way of righting itself. You can't go on living without looking over your shoulder, at least not without me." There was a pleasure in his voice, the kind that only comes when death has stared you in the face but turned away.

"We will take the back stairs to your office. It's

Shattered Night

far enough away from the fire to buy us time. You will send out a message to every leader, every news source, every person you can think of letting them know that you have killed both Cain Foley and Jordyn Dailey." He looked at the woman he would die for, and almost had several times. "No one will look for you in hopes of finding me."

"What do I get in return?" Keegan asked.

"You get to live."

Jordyn scowled at him, undoubtedly reeling that the monster in front of her was about to slip away. "Take your belt off and put it on one of the other guards, and fast. Everyone here will think you were lost to the flames. You'll have a chance to start over, somewhere else. But be different, be someone else, or I swear to God we will find you and finish what we started here today."

Keegan hesitated. "There are keys to a truck upstairs by the telegraph. After I send the messages out, you will ensure my safe passage to that vehicle?"

Cain and Jordyn looked at each other, then Cain spoke. "Yes. Jordyn will move the vehicle back behind the village so you won't be seen and I will stay with you. You will make it out of here alive, that I can promise you."

***

Marcus Keegan took the getaway truck that Cain had provided and sped down the dirt road toward the highway. Whether Cain would ever know it or not, he had beaten him once again. Yes, he'd accepted Cain's deal and had to fake his own death, but he had lived, and that was the best victory of all. With a promise of a future, he headed toward a town in the middle of nowhere. It had been last on his list when he'd planned on expanding his empire, so, fortunately, he hadn't visited before, and wouldn't be recognized. The place was surrounded by nothing but flat farmlands and pastures where people had begun to raise livestock again. He would blend in, and he would do it gladly.

Until an opportunity arose, and when it did, he would seize it with both hands.

It was a month before she revealed herself. She let him get settled, living in the shadows, existing on a few dollars here and there from bartending jobs in places that a man like Keegan wouldn't go to. She let him build a home, in a small apartment building that housed mostly ranchers and tradesmen who were just passing through, selling their wares and disappearing again.

He was cooking on the stove when he heard her. As he turned off the burner, he said. "How did you find me?"

"I never lost you," Jordyn said.

Keegan smiled wryly as he turned around, scoffing to himself for not suspecting it. "You were in the truck the whole time." He gave her a nod, surprisingly, out of respect. "Clever girl."

He took the soup he had heated up and walked toward the couch, a spoon in hand. "Mind if I finish my last meal? I'd imagined it would be more refined than chicken and stars, but who am I to be picky?" Jordyn nodded, and he sat down, the vinyl fabric squealing under his weight. "So, Cain broke his word for once. Moving down in the world I see. Finally willing to slither off of the moral high ground he seems so fond of."

"Cain said *he* can't kill you. He didn't say a thing about me." She ran her hand across a shelf on the wall facing the couch. "Lovely little home you've built here. Too bad this is the last time you will ever see it." She paused. "Micah and I could have had a nice little setup like this someday, maybe a couple kids." Slowly, she took her gun out of her holster and took the safety off, cradling the weapon in her hands. "But you couldn't have that, could you? You wouldn't. God forbid someone else found some happiness."

He looked at her. "It wasn't anything personal, my dear, just business. Your husband was a means to an end, nothing more. I did not set out to destroy your life, it merely happened."

"I believe that, actually. But I also believe that though that wasn't your true goal, you didn't care who you had to destroy along the way. The rest of us, Micah, my mother…they were all just casualties of war to you…one that didn't need to happen in the first place."

Keegan put down the bowl of soup, setting it gently on the end table next to him, then folded his hands in his lap. "Shall we get on with it then? My soup is only lukewarm and I've grown tired of this." He crossed his legs. "Would you like me to pass on a message for you? Tell…Michael is it?"

Jordyn couldn't tell if he had genuinely forgotten her husband's name, or if he was just trying to provoke her. The fact was, it didn't matter. Because as she pulled the trigger, Keegan's skull became a fog of pink mist.

She collapsed on the ground, expecting some sort of peace to envelope her. She thought something would melt through her, sending the pain she had felt since the day she had watched the life slip from Micah's lungs out into the atmosphere.

It didn't.

As she got up and took a deep breath, looking for the relief that wasn't there one last time, she spotted a window in the back of Keegan's apartment. Stepping over him, she walked toward it and stared down at the people below. She watched them for several moments. A husband whispered in his wife's ear, making her smile. A little girl, not much older than McKenzie was when Jordyn first met her, played catch with a boy while wearing a glove that was too big for her. Watching their happiness made an ache worse than anything she had felt before surge through her to the very center of her soul. It was supposed to be over, but as she turned away from the window, she realized why the relief she so desperately needed didn't come.

She wasn't finished yet.

THE END

Acknowledgments

Writing this series has been one of the best journeys of my life and there are several people that helped make it that way. Mom, you always have and always will be my best marketing person and my biggest cheerleader. Thank you for reading my work more than any other person on the planet (other than myself of course)! Dad, thank you for always telling me that part of the game is not quitting the game. Sometimes you just have to outlast all the obstacles. J.J., you are always proud of me, no matter what, and I can't tell you how much I appreciate it. And Madelyn, my beautiful daughter. Thank you for the fact that a smile from you makes all the hard writing days a joy regardless of what's going on at my desk. Lydia at Limitless, your endless patience with my endless questions has been such a blessing. To my literary manager J.D., thank you for believing in my work and letting me come on this fabulous movie-making adventure with you. Robin, thank you for your encouragement and positivity.

About the Author

Renee N. Meland is an avid writer and reader of speculative fiction. She is thrilled to say that The Extraction List Series is in development for film by 5x5 Productions. When she is not writing, she is gardening or learning a new recipe. This is her fifth novel.

Facebook:
https://www.facebook.com/pages/Renee-N-Melands-Books/311899338826241

Twitter:
https://twitter.com/Reneenmeland

Website:
https://www.reneenmeland.com/

Instagram:
https://www.instagram.com/authorreneenmeland/

Goodreads:
http://www.goodreads.com/author/show/8194285.Renee_N_Meland

Join our Reader Group on Facebook and don't miss out on meeting our authors and entering epic giveaways!

Join today! *"Where reading a book is your first step to becoming limitless…"*

https://www.facebook.com/groups/LimitlessReading/

Made in the USA
Columbia, SC
12 November 2018